BUD SMITH

DOUBLE BIRD

maudlinhouse.net
twitter.com/maudlinhouse

ISBN 13: 978-0-9994723-7-8
ISBN-10: 0-9994723-7-2

Double Bird

Cover painting by Tyler Gross
Illustration on pg. 144 by Michael Seymour Blake
Illustration in 'About the Author' by Michael Seymour Blake

For the Grantham family.

1

Tiger Blood 9
Gling Gling Gling 13
Tuesday 19
Agartha 23
Leaving Las Vegas 33
Junior in the Tunnels 35
Birthday! 39
The Moon 49
rek-rek-kek-kek-kek 59
Random Balloons 63
American Flags 71

2

Wolves 75
31,028 79

3

Goblin 83
Schwimps 91
Good Gravy 99
Everybody's Darlin' 103
Jangle Bell 109
E - A - D - G - B -E 115
Everyone (Everyone, Everyone, Everyone) 121
The Wasteland Motel 127
Franklin 135
When I Touch Your Face 137

4

Rabbit Driving Cellphone 145

5

Only the Gentle 149
Temporarily Here 155
Forks, Knives, Spoons 161
Roast Beast 165
Double Bird 169
Blue, Blue, Electric Blue 173
The Lost Girls 177
JANT 181
Pentagram 185
The Paralyzer 189
Rye 199
Enoch 203
Scanner 209
RIP 215
Boss 219
Freebird 225

1

Tiger Blood

I MEET A GIRL ON OK CUPID AND THE FIRST DATE goes well enough. We sit in a red booth with folds like a heart sliced open and stare at each other, sipping icy beverages, smiling the way you should at these things.

She says, "I've got tiger blood."

"Oh? Like what do you mean? In a jar or something?"

"No, in my body."

"I'm crazy too," I say. "I once swallowed a handful of gravel. Helps me digest."

"Like a pelican," she says, nodding, understanding.

Jackie. Her name is Jackie. Jackie with her hair gelled back.

I grin and have spinach in between most teeth (I see it in a mirror later) but she doesn't say anything. Now, she's chill. I stir my iced tea. I wish we were plastered. I wish we were plastered and having sex, no condom, in the back of my pickup truck parked in the shade behind the plaza.

We're in recovery. That happened by accident, you know. It almost always does.

"What kind of gravel was it?" she asks. "Sharp red rocks? Blue like jetty stone? River pebbles?"

"Ah come on, I was just screwing around. I didn't swallow any gravel."

She sits up straight.

"Well why would you say something that wasn't true?"

"You started it."

"I really do have tiger blood, though."

"Really do, uh huh."

"I'll show you."

We're sober and I have car insurance right now and a current registration and even have a driver's license and this is America and I really like this girl and want to impress her so we leave the restaurant without paying and break into the science lab at the community college.

We are working in the dark so as not to alert the watchman. Working by the miraculous LED light of cellphone. She plugs the microscope into the wall.

It glows.

"I don't usually do things like this on the first date."

"It's cool," I say.

"Slice me open, but be gentle."

I want her to like me, so I don't hesitate, I drag a scalpel across her forearm and she catches a droplet of red on a perfect little glass slide and pushes it underneath the microscope, into the only shine in the room.

"Okay, take a look."

I lean down and look.

Well look at that. She doesn't have happy red inner tube ringlets or plasma lifesavers or even globs of shivering crimson.

She really does have tigers.

Bengal tigers, I think, and they are running around on the slide in slow motion. The tigers chase each other. And play. And some yawn wide, lay down and sleep. And others are already sleeping. Countless tigers. In her blood. A sea of them, bounding and rolling, and attacking, and screwing, and fighting, and jumping over each other and licking their own tails and paws.

It was incredible. She was incredible. At least in this one way.

But as it goes, we didn't last very long.

We had just another date after that.

I took her roller skating.

I must not have impressed her very much with my roller skating.

And I could not pull magic out of the unknown.

And I could not cause any dark room to glow the way that room did with the night watchman lost roaming other halls.

And I could not vomit gravel like a bird does before leaping up, sailing away over an endless canyon.

Gling Gling Gling

A WOMAN TAPPED THE CARTOON CHERRIES AND teal diamonds on the cellphone screen as she steered through town with her knee. The game went gling gling gling and then there was a bursting sound, meaning she'd won. She looked up as a man in a camel-colored jacket wandered into the street on a diagonal. The woman hit him with the car and then stomped the brakes.

He'd flown into a pile of cardboard boxes and discarded fake floral arrangements outside the florist shop and was now just crumpled there, wheezing and bleeding.

In her shock, she forgot to put the car in park. As she jumped out to run to the man, the car with its dented steel and blown out glass kept rolling down the hill towards the foggy sea. But no one saw any of this. And soon she was crouching at his side.

"I messed up!"

He spun his lacerated face and his bright blue eyes looked so familiar. But the mouth was full of blood and the mouth of a stranger.

She wasn't crying, but he said, "Don't cry. It's okay. I hit somebody with my car last week. I didn't even stop. Just kept going."

"I'm so so sorry," she said.

He wiped his mouth with his coat and said, "I'm sorry, too. My phone went flying. Can you get it?" He motioned up the sidewalk and the woman stood like there'd been a gunshot at the beginning of a race. The final wishes of a dying man, to tweet about his simple fleeting life or to post a final goodbye selfie. Maybe retweet something religious to ensure entry into Heaven.

His phone had a cracked screen and she apologized again when she handed it to him, but all he said was, "I'm the dumbass who should have been looking at the —" He tapped his phone and finished a text he'd been trying to send to his kid.

"I'll call an ambulance ..." she said.

"Nah." He hacked red. "Don't call an ambulance. I don't have health insurance and that's too much money."

"I get it, I don't have health insurance, either."

"Help me up. This is embarrassing."

She held his hand. It was already blue.

He kept bleeding and bleeding. Most of it was from somewhere in the middle. She made him sit up, and he had the bright idea to stuff fake flowers where the blood was coming from. An entire bouquet of plastic roses and artificial ivy, pushed into his wound. She wrapped him in bubble wrap around the torso. There was twine in a trash can nearby. She tied him up tight like a package. He said, "I'm fine now. I really am. It was nice to meet you. Which way is the cemetery? I'll just go die now."

"It's up there," she said, squinting past the sun, motioning upward through the steep town.

He laughed. "I've never walked uphill in my life. Why start now?" He shook her hand. Did a little bow.

"No. No. I'll fucking drive you ... fuck fuck fuck fuck."

They got to their feet, and she looked back but the car was gone. She ran down the hill, now in a panic. Cars were parked on either side of the street and her car had plummeted down the hill like a pinball, pounding into Chryslers and Toyotas, Hondas and even a Maserati flying an Italian flag. Her car had been stopped somehow by a parking meter, that was now bent back, way back, twisted like a noodle.

The sun came out from behind a cloud. The day was revealed, all shadows gone poof; here were these ordinary people stuck in permanent lightning flash. Sweat rolled down her face. The dying man inched down the street, perfectly cool. He was weak and shaking, but perfectly cool. The hem of his coat was now dripping red. She called for him. "Wait there, you stubborn sonofabitch! I'll come to you! It'll be alright."

She was able to get her car in reverse. But the parking meter ripped out of the cement and remained embedded in the nose of the car as she drove up the hill. For a little while there were sparks but the sparks stopped after the asphalt ground down the bottom of the parking meter. Then everything was fine, was normal.

They felt guilty about the damages. So they scribbled quick notes, and left the notes stuck to all the cars, except the black sedan that was his, crumpled worse of all, emblems ripped off. He wrote notes on scraps of paper from a notebook he carried in his breast pocket. She jotted her apologies on lavender Post-it notes that were kept above her sun visor. The man left his contact information on some of the notes. The woman left her contact information on the rest of the notes. They stuck the notes under windshield wipers, to passenger side windows, on gas caps. They drove away.

"Actually, besides the funeral home, I have a few errands I was trying to run," he said. "Can you help me?"

"Anything you need."

"I don't wanna mess up your day though."

He put his head back on the headrest and stopped breathing. She shook him as she drove and said, "Hey! Hey! Hey!"

The man shuddered and his arm shot out. He turned the radio on. He shouted over the noise of the radio, "What are your plans for the afternoon?"

She turned the radio down.

"On my way to a job interview," she said. "I'm almost late." She pointed at the clock. "But that doesn't matter. We should be getting you to a doctor."

"I don't do doctors. Take me to the bank," he said. "I want to deposit my paycheck. Then, I don't care, we can go to your interview. If you need a reference, you can give them my cellphone number."

"They might call two weeks from now though. You won't be around in two weeks."

He laughed, "You just answer my phone and speak on your own behalf. Pretend you're me." He handed her his phone.

"That's nice of you, how much was the phone, I want to reimburse you. Or your estate or whatever. Your kids …"

"It came with the phone plan. De nada. It's nothing. You're sweet. Speaking of my estate, how patient are you? Could you sit through a game of tee ball tomorrow night? My kid has tee ball and I'll be … Can you?"

"Of course!" she said. "I love tee ball. I take full responsibility. They'll call me Mrs. Tee Ball, okay?"

"Make my kid wear sunscreen."

She nodded.

The man refused to go through the drive thru so the woman helped him into the bank. He couldn't walk. His organs must have been shutting down and his legs didn't work now. She held onto him at the counter, supporting him as he filled out the deposit slip and passed it to the clerk behind the counter in the flowery dress shirt, who insisted on giving them three bottles of mineral water and a ridiculous amount of lollipops.

Next they went to the post office and sent off a couple Easter cards. The envelopes had started out pink and only one of them had gotten slick with blood. That envelope was now shit brown, and the postal clerk refused to take any money for the stamp. This one is on the house, sir.

The man also refused to sit in the car when the woman went in to her job interview. She popped the trunk and found two beach towels in the back and wrapped them around him to cover up the mess that his body was making through the bubble wrap and twine and artificial flowers. He was starting to smell. It was his idea to be doused with air freshener from a forgotten bottle next to the spare tire.

Even though she was late and even though she had a dying man with her, the job interview went pretty well. It looked like she'd get the position. The only part of the interview she had thought was a touch too personal, was when her future boss(?) had pried into whether or not she had children. She'd tried to skate around the fact that she medically could not have children of her own, and the man frowned, as if—one demerit. But when she said she did not smoke cigarettes, and did not feel the need to see much of the world, and therefore that meant less vacation time, he'd nodded happily, like, alright—two bonus gold stars next to your name, well done. Gling gling gling.

On the paperwork for references, she wrote the name she'd seen the dying man put on the bank deposit slips. She wrote his cellphone number. It felt good to have a friend in the world, someone to count on.

When she went back into the lobby he was dead.

The receptionist hadn't noticed. One of the other job applicants walked in, late for his interview anyway, and made a whole scene about it, like he'd get brownie points for noticing or something. But the woman dragged the dead man out to her car. She softly wept as she drove farther down the hill. Directionless on a sunny afternoon.

She noticed some bloody books had fallen out of his coat. She reached down at his feet and grabbed them. Library books. She'd return them for him. A book about black holes. A novel about Nazi gold in a sunken submarine, treasure hunters scuba diving down to steal it, but you know, there was also this mutated nuclear warhead octopus. How preposterous. She threw the books out the window into oncoming traffic.

The dead man's cellphone began to ring on the console.

She picked it up.

"Hello?"

"Hello, I'm calling because you are qualified for a free vacation ..."

The woman screamed. The scream turned into a shriek of sorrow and then uncontrollable tears. The telemarketer said, "Everything okay?"

"Oh my god, I'm so sorry—guy you're calling is kaput. I'm looking at him right now. He's no longer of the mortal coil and he's in my car."

The telemarketer stuttered, "In in in your ca-car? Who is this?"

"I hit him with my car, d-e-a-d. I'm so sorry!"

"Lady, just stop it."

Cars turned in front of her on the boulevard that went down towards the sea.

"I hit him with my car ..."

"You said that, yeah. Okay, you're on the no call list now. You've made your point."

"But I—" She was out of words. The telemarketer blabbed on about the free vacation.

A park flashed by. Kids were playing soccer in the park. She stopped at a red light. A cop pulled up next to her. He looked in the car. The car was wrecked. There was a parking meter stuck to the hood. There was a dead body in her passenger seat. She was on the phone.

The cop rolled down his window and leaned over. He was hot about it. He looked like a bull in a Bugs Bunny cartoon. Red faced and steam coming out of his nostrils.

She hung up the phone.

The cop changed into a smiling boy. His eyes became kind. He gave her a big thumbs up.

The cop looked twice each way and then rolled through the red light.

Traffic swarmed around her, she remained motionless. She ran her hands through the dead man's hair, clearing it away from his forehead.

She did a k-turn and headed back up the hill, away from the sea, towards the cemetery.

Her car was shaking and she wasn't sure she would make it. But she had Triple A and if Triple A had to tow her to the cemetery then they would just have to. She didn't know how much it cost to bury a person. She would finance it. She would charge a deposit to her credit card. She'd get a second job if she did indeed get the first job. Tax returns were coming.

In the parking lot of the cemetery, his phone buzzed again. A text from the dead man's kid, who was at school and needed a lift.

The woman texted the dead man's kid, I LOVE YOU, BE THERE SOON. GIVE ME SOME TIME. STAY IN THE SHADE.

Tuesday

THE SEASHELL SPOKE TO ME. ALL NICE THINGS. Don't alert the guards or anything, hehehe. The seashell was orange and white and encouraging.

While I slouched at the kitchen table, the seashell gave me predawn peptalks, "Big day today, bet you'll do good."

"Big day? I'm a janitor."

"Oh—please quit that job."

"Sure. But I think I do alright there."

"No one mops like you."

"Thank you."

"But, don't get comfortable, update your resumé."

"I will," I promised the seashell.

"I've seen your potential. I watch your dreams. Did you know that? They flicker in my shell like a movie. Last night's was wonderful."

Its voice was sharp, though it held back and tried to make itself sound so soft.

"I don't remember. What happened in the dream?"

"Such beautiful things. Your reality sucks. But you have the most beautiful dreams. That's why I love you."

I sipped my coffee. I'm no good with compliments. After work, if I came home and needed someone to talk to, I knew I could always count on the seashell. As a joke, the seashell would even mimic the sea, the waves, seagulls, but it would sound like if me or you were just doing it as a gag.

"What's your name?"I said.

"You don't wanna know," it said.

We left it at that.

On Tuesdays, we had Quiz Night. I liked Quiz Night mostly because I always won. The seashell would ask me question after question, and I always knew the answer.

"Who invaded Spain in 1814?"

"Napoleon."

"What is the strongest muscle in the human body?"

"The tongue."

"How far is the moon in miles?"

"Right now?" I looked out the window, through a sliver between two brick walls. I could see the moon up there, a golden egg, formed many years ago when this planet was struck by an asteroid as big as Mars.

"I'm waiting ..."

"Far," I said. "The moon is far."

"238,855 miles," the seashell said. "But I'll accept 'far' as a correct answer."

I don't know when I found the seashell. It was just in my hand one day. And I can't remember when I started to carry the seashell with me everywhere, cupped in both hands like the Holy Grail. While we passed about it made comments on the scenery, like some kind of tour guide.

"Nice lawn. Lush."

And— "Look at those beautiful clouds."

And— "Check out that mailbox. All those poor seashells glued to it. Trapped. Ha! Some people have quite an evil soul."

Velcro'd to the dashboard, the seashell gave directions as I drove. "Turn left here, turn left here, okay, go about a quarter mile and then veer right straight into the ocean."

"Hey, nice try."

It didn't like to go into my pocket. It'd stab me. There'd be blood. I couldn't blame it. Sometimes it's hard to see your lessers overtake you. But I needed my hands, so we compromised, and I began to wear the seashell around my neck, like an oversized, iridescent amulet.

People thought I was a mystic.

I got strange looks while I mopped at the facility.

As I pushed the cart around the grocery store, the seashell would suggest things that I'd never thought to try; fresh tarragon, beets, natural pink sea salt from the Himalayas, watercress.

Life evolves. Darkness got longer as the days were smothered in belts of fog. This is just about the time the guilt trips began.

"We should get going," it'd say, every night interrupting my sleep.

I'd tap it on the night stand, as if it had a snooze button.

"Stop that! Pack your bags, let's go."

"Where?" I'd ask.

"You know where."

"Back into the sea?"

"You said it, not me."

"I'd die in the sea."

"You wouldn't die in the sea. You'd be fine. You came from that place. I remember you when you were just a little baby."

"Shhh, please."

"You were so tiny," it said, "you fit right inside me and you were safe and warm and nothing had strong enough teeth to break me, so you were fine. We were all the way at the bottom of the bottom of the bottom of the bottom. Can we go back?"

"No. I can never go back. Things have changed."

"You got too big for me," the seashell said.

"I'm here now," I said. "I'll never leave you again."

But it wouldn't stop weeping. Its weeping echoed through the place inside itself it claimed I had once lived.

"You wouldn't remember, you didn't have a brain yet, just a nervous system."

I had to move the seashell into the kitchen, hidden under a glass cake lid to deaden the sound. I slept with a duck feather pillow over my head. It wouldn't stop singing.

Last Tuesday there was a very bad accident. We were in the middle of a harsh argument. The seashell had learned I was moving to the top of a mountain. Unacceptable. I pointed the car towards the boardwalk. I guess it could smell the salt air and knew what was next, so it just got more and more desperate. It was shaking and shrieking and hissing at me.

We were hit by a garbage truck that'd blown a red light as we were crossing the street, screaming at each other. Both my legs were shattered. My arm broken in six spots. My skull bruised like a watermelon about to go in the dumpster. The seashell was smashed to dust. The wind scattering the speckled powder away.

Yet, just last night, while the ward was quiet, and the drugs hummed in me, I heard its voice say, "What's the capital of Venezuela?"

I tired to ignore it.

"What's the capital of Venezuela?" it said louder.

"Caracas," I said.

"You still got it, you're so smart."

The night nurse peeked in. "What was that?"

"What?" I said.

She said, "Did you just yell out?"

I said, "No. No. Hehehe. I'm fine."

Agartha

THEY WANTED TO REPOSSESS MY DOG.

I'd defaulted on my student loans and the creditors sent a letter that they were coming to take her. That was finally the thing that sent me away from your society.

Very carefully I did not answer the phone. When someone came to the door I held my breath. They knocked on the door and we ducked farther into the house, as she started woofing. I put my hand on the nape of her neck, where the collar would be if I was cruel. I said, "Shhhhhh."

Her coat was slick and shiny because I'd been feeding her avocados and eggs to ready her for our journey, our escape. Her fur felt good on my palm, there was no fear. Someone had stolen my dog once before, I had to rescue her from the thieves. They'd beaten me, left me for dead on the frozen ground. But in the end it'd all worked out. I'd gotten my dog back. She's faithful to a fault.

The shadow outside on the porch leaned on the glass with cupped hands, trying to peek into my house. But the power had gone off ever since I'd lit the bomb off in my basement and blew a hole in the floor wide and deep.

"Everything alright in there?" My dog growled. The person left.

They'd already towed my car out of the driveway. But it was alright, I'd been preparing and wouldn't need a car where I was going.

Did you know the earth is hollow? Did anybody ever tell you? You can go and live inside this hollow earth beneath your feet if you like. There are many passageways, many ways in, but most are narrow. You'll love it down there, the cost of living is lower. You don't need a car or car insurance or gasoline or oil changes. It's amazing what you can learn on the Internet.

My dog growled again, but I shushed her and we moved farther into the house.

Someone was knocking on the back door now. I peeked around the corner. Through the window in the door I could see another shadowed outline in the daylit world.

I whispered to my dog, "It was a mistake to buy all this knowledge and then to try and sell the knowledge back to someone else. That's the way a curse is sometimes passed on—save yourself from the curse by cursing someone else."

And by light of my cellphone flashlight we opened the door to the basement and began our adventure downward.

My suitcase was at the mouth of the crater, stuffed with survival gear and food: beef jerky and black beans, dehydrated milk and instant coffee, fig bars and sunflower seeds, nine gallons of water.

This was all tucked into a suitcase with fantastic rolling caster wheels.

The bomb hadn't opened the passageway to Agartha. I had to jackhammer through another seven feet of rock, but finally I broke through and exposed the entrance to one of the tunnels.

Now I threw my suitcase into that subterranean passageway. Then jumped down into the tunnel myself. With a whistle my dog took the leap of faith too. I caught her like a touchdown. She'd follow me anywhere. I pushed the button and our lantern lit up. We began to walk through the crude tunnel: roots and dripping water from above, mineral stink, pebbles falling here and there, the rumblings of vehicles.

With 1% battery life on the phone left and a signal so weak, I stopped and sent my brother this brief email:

DOUBLE BIRD

Hey,

Set off a bomb in my house and I climbed into the crater. Won't be at your place for Thanksgiving. Tell Michelle I am sorry. If you want, there is a jackhammer that fell into the hole, seven feet, if you get it out and bring it back to Hardware Heaven, you can get my deposit back. It's $100. Love you, don't follow.

Your bro

I put my phone in my pocket and it buzzed. It was a message from a person I'd met on a dating service. we'd gone on three dates but hadn't had sex. We had no spark to be honest. Sometimes love can keep you tethered to civilization, but I didn't have that love, so leaving civilization was easy breezy.

Date: Hi, I'm at the restaurant. R U here?

Me: I'm sorry! forgot about our date! actually I'm descending through the crust of the earth tonight ...

Date: what does that mean?

Me: moving, changing careers

Date: why?

Me: uh, don't wanna be an adjunct professor anymore, don't wanna teach creative writing ... have decided to venture underground, legit.

Date: Srsly?

Me: so I won't be dating for awhile probs, but it's no reflection on you

Date: fuck youuuuuuuuu

I tried to reply again but I'd already been blocked. I wanted to tell my date that there are such things as lizard people, UFOs, and cities hidden deep below the unsuspecting surface. I wanted to comfort my date so my date could understand that I wasn't just rejecting them, I was rejecting them and everything else they knew.

The first day, we walked deeper. The walls were muddy and in some spots rubbing against my shoulders. At one point, I felt very claustrophobic and turned sideways. I took my dead cellphone out of my pocket and shoved the cellphone into the mud. It disappeared with a sucking sound and I smiled, relieved. Later that day, I tossed my wallet and my car keys/house keys into a bubbling pool of water that smelled like rotten eggs and sorrow. That too made me feel better. Lighter and heroic. That night was cold and of course dark outside of the lantern light. I wrapped a wool blanket around myself and lay with my dog beneath stalagmites dotted orange and yellow with fungus. Time existed only on a wristwatch, but each second that clicked on reminded me that I could find solace in forgetting all about human history, because where I was headed, human history didn't have any clout.

That night I had a dream that my house had been loaded onto a flatbed truck and the house had been driven back to the bank and the bank ate my house. All the bankers came out of the bank and ripped off a piece of my house and in the blinding sunshine, the bankers laughed and ate and grew fat while they ate my house. They ate everything I owned, and in the dream I felt better and better.

They ate through the walls of the house and into the house and ate every book I had ever read. Each book they ate cleared my mind in the dream. And then they ate my clothes and my photo albums and even my mother's and father's ashes on the mantel, and that made me feel good too. The bankers ate into my bedroom and consumed the pile of bills on my nightstand that I wasn't paying anyway. They ate my checkbook and the notebook where I kept all my secret passwords. They ate the calendars from the wall. They completely freed me of everything. I woke up so happy.

I woke my dog and in the lantern light, I fed her crackers and canned chicken and the last of the baby carrots.

We walked on. The path a winding downward slope. Occasionally, I found a couple steps that were carved with obvious chisel marks. Man-made. At one point that day, I found a graffiti on the wall in pink spray paint: HOW COULD THEY SEE ANYTHING BUT SHADOWS?

Farther up, there was this, A.A WUZ HERE 8/2/83 And then below that: SO WAS MONEY 9/19/01. Besides occasional litter, this was the only sign of American life I saw, unless some of the swastikas I found were painted by Americans, which they are known to do from time to time.

Later that day, my dog and I came across great underground pools of water, steaming and seeming fresh, but I didn't let my dog go in the water and I didn't go in either. I'd just seen a news report about a person who had climbed inside a hot spring at Yellowstone National Park and melted from the water, dying almost instantly, disappearing almost just as fast.

Instead of going in the water, I poured some of the bottled water I'd bought at Food Universe and towed along in my suitcase into my hand. I let my dog drink from my hand.

I said, "Sometimes I think knowledge is just a weight that crushes a person. The more you know, the more the weight crushes down on you. It might save your life, but it also makes you miserable."

My dog looked up at me and I wondered how joyous it must be to only know a couple words.

I said, "Did you know that ants can carry ten times their own weight? Did you know that ants have the IQ of an ant, not very smart. Ants do fine, they can carry a lot of weight. Ants are very happy and they have all the things an ant needs to live a full insect life. I can't even afford new sneakers. I just glued my sole back on and now I am ready to walk for awhile."

After my big speech to my silent dog, I too was silent for days. As if I'd taken a vow. And as if that vow was powering the journey itself.

The path opened into a great hall of stone crooks and crevices that served no seeming purpose as we walked through it for hours, forever stepping down farther and farther into the earth. This natural amphitheater, empty, except for the echo of my footsteps and the panting of my dog.

Some people will tell you there is no chance whatsoever that the earth is hollow. I am well acquainted with those kinds of people. I used to see them all the time on message boards. I used to argue with them all the time online. But each time I tried to fight them and their ignorance, all I discovered from my own research was that there are so many things beyond the narrow scope of the human mind ... I'd click a link and find some other truth. Satellite photos of massive holes seen in the north pole, shot from space. A respected air force pilot who had flown his plane into one of these openings at the pole and had seen firsthand, vast ranges of underground mountains, rivers, a purple sea itself, cities unlike any he'd ever encountered topside. One piece of truth leads to another and then another and ...

I first learned about Agartha from a video clip I found online. An astronaut in zero gravity was playing around with a bubble of water. The earth itself is nearly 75% water, so a water droplet is actually a 125% perfect representation of the earth.

The astronaut had some contraption that mimicked the exact rotation of the earth around the sun. And the bubble of water hung suspended in the 'orbit'. Ah, look at that. How beautiful. The astronaut then pointed out that air bubbles inside the orbiting water droplet were forming and being pushed to the center of the water droplet. The orb, through rotation on its neat little axis, had created a hollow in its own middle. Next part of the video the astronaut showed how earth was formed with molten lava, just solid lava, whole thing, and as it spun in space, it cooled, and the air bubble that formed in the middle, well that was called Agartha. Isn't science so cool?

I'm not going to even get into the part of the YouTube video where the astronaut dropped little specks of leaves in the water droplet to represent the continents. But that does sum up and match my feelings when thinking about life on earth.

Life on terrestrial earth is like lying in a pile of sloppy, wet leaves that smell horrible.

The third day, it began to warm up. The reason it began to warm up is not because the center of the earth is a molten core of lava like you've been told by book-learned dummies. It's because there is a blue sun in the center of the earth, and I was walking towards it with my dog.

And on the fourth day I felt comfortable enough to let you know that my dog's name is Enoch. She's a good dog. She's kind and not too bright, but her sense of smell and sense of direction are impeccable. So when there was a branch in the tunnel, I always felt comfortable letting Enoch pick the way.

That fifth night we stopped as usual in our passage and I sat and ate and fed Enoch some of our beef jerky and the last of our Honey Nut Cheerios.

The lantern began to get dim, its battery fading, we wouldn't have much more light.

"We'll be stumbling around in the dark like ignoramuses soon. Get ready for that new way of life. Lucky for us I packed other batteries."

But then there was the sound of birds and I was stunned to see them flutter past us. Enoch leapt up and snapped her jaw but the birds were small and fast.

It was then I knew for sure that we were headed the right direction. The birds were trying to get back up to your sky. After that Enoch didn't even have to pick which way we went at the splits. I knew just to be walking towards the birds, going the opposite way. Going against common animalistic sense to see the blue skies. To feel the sweet wind. To let the rain wash the dust from their wings.

That night, just before we were ready to stop traveling, we came to a branch in the tunnel with a sign that read CITY TO RIGHT, CANYON TO LEFT. In the direction of the sign that said canyon, I saw a set of stone steps. Enoch didn't want to go that way, but I persuaded her to go up the steps with me. At the top there was a small hatch, bolted closed, but not locked. I lifted the hatch and blue light filled the tunnel. I opened the hatch the rest of the way and climbed the steps to the top. Enoch wouldn't follow, she stayed in the tunnel growling.

"It's okay," I said. But I wasn't sure, myself.

I checked my watch again, and was sure it was ten o'clock at night, but there was the blue sun, right above me, dead center between two sheer faced stone walls, yellow and white, that looked unscalable. This sun did not rise. This sun did not set. It was forever hovering in place. The stone faced canyon walls were smooth but covered in spots high up with what seemed like ordinary ivy. I looked back down the hatch, "Enoch, please come up here..." But she wouldn't.

"Suit yourself, I'll be right back."

I walked onward down the path. All I saw was stone and ivy. But the farther away from the hatch I got, the more I lost my wits. Then I saw something coming my way on the path ahead and I froze. Something the size of a boot, bouncing in quick leaps. The creature was covered in fur that was dragging on the ground. Protruding tusks. Antlers. It realized I was there and it lifted its head to look me in the eye. That's when I lost my shit and turned back and sprinted towards the hatch.

Once I was in the tunnel again with Enoch I felt better. I sat on the steps and calmed myself. Enoch was down on the floor, drinking some drippings that had fallen from the ceiling of the tunnel.

I lifted the hatch again and peeked out. There were more of those creatures up there. I counted three now. They were sniffing the ground and hopping along.

I lowered the hatch and bolted it closed again. I said to Enoch, "Okay, girl, you were right about the canyon. It's not safe there. The canyon is filled with rabbits from outer space...inner space...whatever. Let's go."

Two more days we walked like that, ignoring branches in the tunnel that went anywhere but towards the city.

I was startled when we suddenly came to the end of the tunnel and there was a wooden door in the center of a block wall marked AGARTHA.

A sign next to the door read, KNOCK LOUD.

I knocked on the door with my knuckles. Nothing. I knocked even harder with my hand like a hammer. Nothing. I began to beat on the door and yell but nothing happened. I smashed the door harder and screamed. I picked up a small boulder and slammed it into the door and screamed even louder.

"Okay! I hear you!" a woman's voice said from the other side of the door.

She unbolted the door and by the time Enoch and I made it through to the other side, the woman was sitting at a desk reading a magazine by candlelight.

"You're not a lizard a person..." I smiled.

"Thanks for noticing," she said. She had a strong German accent. There was another door at the end of the room she was in.

"I'm looking for a new world to live in, is it through that door?"

She looked at the door and considered it. "I like it, I guess. You have to work though. Will you work?"

"If I have to, I will."

"You do, yeah. Way it goes. What kinds of skills do you have?"

"I was a teacher," I said. "A college professor."

"Oh," she frowned. "Okay. Can I see some proof?"

I reached in my back pocket and pulled out my university ID card. I also had my diploma. I handed the two things over.

She looked at Enoch. I said, "She doesn't bite."

She said, "She's got teeth, she bites. Any fool knows that."

The woman scowled, and handed back the diploma.

"We don't value knowing things. What'd you make a year up there?"

"Negative fifteen thousand dollars."

"Happily, there are no teaching jobs here. Most top side college professors have become trench diggers and now perform heavy manual labor. Can you peel potatoes? Have you ever done any janitorial work? What about burying the dead?"

I folded my diploma back up and slid it back into my pocket.

"Bury the dead? I have a college degree," I said.

"So you think this work is beneath you?"

I laughed.

"Physically speaking," she said. "You're at the bottom of the world. If you want to go in, you'll have to swing a pickaxe, you'll have to gather mushrooms, you'll have to sheer wooly mice and work the shoots that drain the oceans for our crops. You will do this work?"

"I'll be valued?"

"You'll be valued, yes." I stared at the closed door just beyond her desk.

"Through that door..." I said. "Is that Hell?"

"Nah, It's a nice place. Not much crime. Just no normal sunshine. Where you came from, was that Hell?"

I shook my head. "I'll mop the netherworld," I said.

"Good. But first, I'll see that you eat that college degree of yours."

I said, "Done."

"I want to see you eat it."

I was hungry anyway. So I took my diploma out of my back pocket, and for this woman, I tore off chunks of my diploma and put each chunk in my mouth. I chewed three times for each chunk of paper and then swallowed. And don't you know, I felt better than ever.

Next up the woman had me fill out paperwork.

I filled it all out in a gleeful scribble. Out came the rubber stamper, she rubbed the stamper on a pad of ink and then slammed the stamper down on my paperwork.

"Welcome to your new life."

As the door opened, a wave of new birds that had been waiting for their chance flew past in a desperate swoosh and Enoch turned her head, tongue hanging out, happily oblivious, watching them fly back into total darkness.

Leaving Las Vegas

DAY 1:

Got a crazy nice rental car (for free) and can't figure out how to get the gas cap open because fancy things are complicated. Now I'm out of fuel and on the side of the road, walking into the darkened trees, smearing mud on myself. I live in the forest now, I'll make a weapon from a simple rock and prosper.

Day 2:

Draped now in animal pelts; deer, raccoon, fox (mimicking movies I saw) I move soundlessly through the brush, gathering berries both to eat and to make stains to paint art. Sometime near dusk my fucking iPhone dies. Of all the things I've lost, I miss beer most.

Day 23:

While swimming in rock pool at hidden waterfall, I realize I've forgotten all the passwords to all the things; my bank account, the garage door, the alarm system, my email account—up on ledge, she has stripped down completely and is smiling as she jack knifes into the biting water, creating not a ripple.

Day 45:

We have moved farther away from the light. The stars become bigger. I cook; she hunts.

Day 100:

decide winter too harsh, make long return to rental car, find encased in thorn vines, impenetrable. manage to smash apart door. have metal now from it to make daggers and better arrows. walk back home, our tracks are those of grizzly feet we cut off and wear. I think it pretty cool, maybe instill fear in others looming in ridges. she hold my hand for first time.

Day 153:

first rains not frozen sky snow earth returns beneath white all gone soon green poking up and we gather it for salad when I joke about something I used to know, haha balsamic vinaigrette, she tilts her head as if I speak of God.

Day 276:

kill … fire ... day ... hmmmm ... child coming ... moon … night … but no wolves

Day ???:

… … …. …

Junior in the Tunnels

SHE'S DISTRESSED. A GLASS BREAKS IN THE SINK. Then another. I walk into the kitchen. "I can't marry you," she says.

Soap suds float in the air, small bubbles. I shut off the hot water.

"It's okay," I say. "So we don't get married. There are billions of people who don't get married."

"Like who?" she says, head down, wiping her wet hands on my chest.

"Like the newscaster on channel three and the lady who stocks the cat food at the grocery store. They're not married."

"They don't even know each other. I know you."

"Okay then, another example. Like, I dunno, the woman who walks that orange dog and the guy hanging off the back of the garbage truck—not to mention, the garbage truck guy sings to her from the back of the truck, that's love."

She laughs, "Don't try to make me laugh." The ring is sitting on the washing machine next to the sink. I pick it up, I put it in my pocket.

"No harm no foul."

Dee was engaged once. Seventeen years ago—which sounds like

a lifetime ago—but I guess that's all how you look at things. What's a lifetime?

His name was Junior. He died in the tunnels beneath the (now abandoned) Mayweather Home. The tunnels connect one wing of the facility to another. Since the Mayweather was closed down by the state, that's where the kids in this town party. It's hard to find how to get in the tunnels, but once you can figure out how to access them, there's no better place to drink underage, to smoke up, to ... I'm a grown ass man, I don't have a need for secret haunted tunnels.

Haunted, yes. That's the other thing.

Dee woke me, heavy rain out the window, slopping in on the floor. The room was semi-dark, but should have been all the way dark, there was some unexplainable ethereal light.

"I promised myself to someone," she said.

"I get that," I said. "I promised myself to Nadine Fincher in the eighth grade. She had the curliest hair on the east coast."

"What happened with you and Nadine?"

"When she hit the ninth grade, she got a hair straightener for her birthday. That was that."

"Well, I don't have curly hair."

"I know, but you dance really fantastic and you tell the best racist jokes I've heard. That's solid gold."

"I'm going to poison you."

"Bring it on."

"What if you died one day, would you want me to be with someone else?"

"I'd want you to be with someone else right now, while I'm much alive if it'd make you happy," I said.

"Wouldn't that kill you?" she said. "Something you should know, every year on his birthday I go and visit him."

"Junior," I say.

She pulled away in the bed.

"You know his name?"

"Guy I work with told me the story."

"I'd rather you not retell the story to me. Tomorrow's his birthday."

"Tell you what, I'll come with you."

"You don't want to go where I'm going."

"I'll even get the cake."

It's a lemon cake with vanilla icing and strawberries. As I carry it, I feel more and more foolish to have not brought forks and a knife of some sort. He'd have been 36. I think my lighter works.

The easiest way to get into the Mayweather is to climb in through a broken window around the side, near the laundry. Dee climbs up on a pile of stumps and slips into the darkened window. Her hands appear, I pass her the birthday cake.

Most of the tiles are smashed. The floor is a nest of clothes, blankets, empty bottles and toys: baby dolls, dominoes, playing cards. Graffiti obscures most everything, as if it were practice for the outside world.

We walk down a long hallway and I don't look in rooms as I pass, because I may not exactly be superstitious, mind you, but I don't want to see anything that invades my dreams if you get my drift.

"Here's the room," she says.

It's a storage room, with a closet wide open. I get distracted by a massive stack of journals from patients. Dee stands there watching me leaf around in some of them. She's being considerate to me, even though I'm not technically being considerate to the privacy of whoever these people are. In one journal, a person writes about a journey on the back of a giant eagle, up to the top of Mount Everest. The end of the world is a very popular topic. But mostly in the journals it seems everyone is obsessed with celebrity. This guy thought he was a famous professional wrestler, a giant. This other guy is Buddy Holly. This girl thought her neighbor was Amelia Earhart.

Dee says, "Okay, library time is over." She smiles and hands me the cake. She climbs in the closet, and moves a rack of clothes out and opens a hidden door.

Now we walk in total darkness. I feel with both hands on a sweaty concrete wall.

"Did you bring a flashlight?"

"They don't work down here," Dee says.

"Well then how do we go?"

"Candle light," she says.

"Well, did you bring any candles? I didn't bring any candles." She flicks a lighter, and begins to light the cake.

I laugh, "Well, except for the 36 in the goddamn cake."

It's a short walk. Five minutes or so. Dee stops. There're initials spray painted on the wall. A date too.

"I did that," she said. "This is where he passed."

She sits Indian-style on the concrete floor. The darkness licks in and pushes out as the candles on the cake flicker.

I sit too.

"Happy Birthday, Junior," she says. "This is my friend, Larry. He has a question to ask you about me. I hope you're here and I hope you're listening. Be brutal, Junior. Be honest. Be severe."

"First," Dee said, "Make a wish."

I open my mouth, confused, is it my wish or his? Then, mouth still agape, I start to ask Junior if it's okay to marry his fiancé. But the candles snuff out.

Birthday!

SHE FOUND A GIANT EGG ON THE LAWN. THIS IS A gag, she thought. She looked around for someone hiding in the woods—she did this smiling, showing lots of white teeth; then crouching, then stabbing her cigarette out in the dirt. Nobody was around. She shook her head, brushed her blonde hair back with an open palm.

Behind her there was a little red house. She was isolated there, deep in that forest. Michelle looked a while longer at the woods, then at the egg, hoping Eric had put it there, coming all this way. She called out, "Hey, you here to bother me? What took you so long? I deserve an apology. You bailed on me."

Something soared through the treetops, cracking branches, pine needles raining down. A massive shadow, gone in a second. Spooked, she picked up the egg—heavier than she thought—and hustled into the house. She propped the egg on the table next to the fridge. Locked the door. Locked the other lock on the door too. Slid to the floor, and laughed, and looked at the egg, and slapped herself in the face, okay, that's enough.

That night, after wine, and bourbon, and three pills, she took a stick of purple lipstick and wrote 'Happy Birthday!' on the speckled shell. When she put her hand to the egg, it was warm. Was comforting somehow. Whatever had abandoned the egg, had given her a gift.

Those were lonely days.

In the morning she drove her diesel into town to get the mail. In the P.O. box was a very serious and official pink letter telling her that her unemployment insurance was cut off. Just a few days prior she'd been denied a disability claim, as if proclaiming, you are not all the way unwell, oh well. Michelle bought a newspaper and searched the jobs section. She kicked a metal pole and hurt her foot, and cursed. Then she crossed the street, limping, and asked for work, again, at the diner, and the bait and tackle shop, the Food Universe. Nothing. So she gave in, dug into her tight jeans and pulled the quarters out, and used the payphone at the gas station, calling home to the farm. She left a message on the answering machine. "Oh hey. It's Michelle. I'll try you guys again soon. I'm doing fine up here. Don't worry about me. Maybe I'll come see you soon? I said I never would. I'm such an asshole. Maybe, I'll come by day after tomorrow? No reason. Would just be nice to see you. Okay, see you then. This is Michelle."

When she got back from town, the table had collapsed. The egg, now quadrupled in size, was still wobbling on the kitchen floor. It'd grown while no one looked. Her 'Happy Birthday!' scrawl was distorted into something else.

The egg shook, and she flinched, falling against the counter, and creating a small avalanche of dirty plates and cups. She sucked her breath in, and decided she was going to change her life. Step one was to get the egg out of the house before it got too big to fit out the front door, and whatever was inside it, made her house its house.

Grunting, and heaving, she rolled the egg into the bed of her pickup truck. And then on the porch she smoked a cigarette, just watching it. There was a chill to the air, so she pulled a sweater over her dress, and watched dusk settle over the valley. For good measure, and for what it was worth, she took a blanket from the closet and placed it over the egg in the bed of the pickup.

In the morning, frost had covered everything. She pulled the blanket back, and placed her hand on the egg. It was even larger now. The size of her. Cool to the touch. She put her ear to it and she heard a coo. She covered it with the blanket again. The sun was warming everything up. The frost disappeared. She drove south. Gravel roads led back into her unhappy past. The pines shrunk into sleeping fields. She eased onto the interstate. In the rearview she saw the egg, jammed tight in the truck bed, unable to roll; she liked that. She didn't want anything bad to happen to it. She took the exit. Barns. Silos. She sped up, and didn't look at her high school on the edge of it all. That's where things had been good, then great, then very bad; senior year punctuated with a breakdown. An attempt to take her own life! She woke up sewed back up, and, ah, here take these pills forever. She knew this was a speed trap. And look, there was the cop. But she was going slow enough. The same billboards. The same dogs running along the edge of the fence line, arf arf arf. Suddenly, she blinked and was all the way home. Her childhood ranch, buttercup yellow. Dad's helicopter sitting there a couple hundred feet from the weeping willow. Mom's nothing sitting nowhere over there by the nada and the zilch and the never mind. But flowers still in the window boxes. Fox glove. Lamb's ear. Mom liked flowers.

At their table, Dad was all denim, as always. After the Air Force, he'd really dug into the whole working the land thing. Michelle guessed he was just all the way tired with the sky, had done enough in it. Mom had new lines on her face, a lifetime of grimacing. She was already shaking her head at Michelle and Michelle hadn't even said a word. They were hard people who believed they knew what right and wrong was.

"How's work?" Dad asked.

"There was a downsize," she said.

"Lost your fancy desk job, eh?" Mom said.

"Yeah, lost my fancy desk job."

Mom laughed, "Everybody wants a soft job. Everybody."

"You were right," Michelle said. "I never should have gone to college. What a dummy."

"You said that, not me," Mom said.

Dad added, "Michelle, don't get cross. You understand how it is. Here we are expecting you to pay us back a little of the money you borrowed, and we're finding out—"

"Actually, I was going to ask to borrow some more."

Mom shook her head no. Dad said, "You're not a little kid

anymore. You're going to have to face your responsibilities. More help, just won't help."

"I am sorry to hear about your job, though," Mom said.

"It's okay," Michelle said, "I've been real busy."

"Job search?" Mom asked.

"Little of that. But, wow, no, not exactly." Michelle couldn't stop laughing.

Dad set his fork down, stared through her. There was always the looming tension—would their daughter crack up again, go back in the facility.

"See, I found an egg," Michelle said in defense, "I've been taking care of it. Boy does it ever take up a ton of my time."

"Taking care of an egg … okay."

"Pass the butter," Mom said. Dad slugged back his milk.

The dalmatian whined under the table. She dropped a handful of raw broccoli. And the dog looked at it, and left in anger. And she laughed some more. It was so funny how she could make no one happy.

After apple pie, there was a small explosion. Truck tires had burst. The axels given out. The egg was so big now the truck bed had buckled out on both sides under the strain of it.

"Nice egg," Dad said. "That was a good truck."

"Junk now," Mom said.

As it turned out, Mom and Dad were going on a three day train ride through the countryside. They had a private cabin and it was supposedly a very romantic getaway. Michelle drove them, in their car, to the train station in the rain. Mom didn't like to leave the ground, and would not fly under any circumstance. Michelle would watch the house while they were gone, since she was already there, stranded there, really. Dad would help her figure something out, he promised, clutching her, hugging her, whispering, "I'm sorry it's so hard, baby."

Alone again in their house, Michelle thawed every steak from the chest freezer, left them on the counter, consumed none.

At dawn, as if the rays of the sun were an alarm clock, the shell began to shake—the shell started to crack.

The racket woke her up. She dressed and rushed down to the

porch just as the beak burst through the shell. Feeling nothing, she watched the bird, roughly her height, wiggle free, chirping blindly.

The sun came up.

Birthday was born full-feathered, never really a chick. Her eyes changed from milk to clear all-seeing jade in only a day. Michelle fed her canisters of oatmeal, fish food, rice. Her wings, rapidly spreading thirty five-feet, wouldn't work yet, but she flapped them in the dust underneath the clothesline, sending the bed sheets sailing. Michelle regretted the wasted steaks.

She drove her parents' car into town, visiting the butcher, coming home with a dead hog in the trunk of the car, as a gift. But when she pulled into the driveway, Birthday was halfway through consuming the dalmatian. The dog's legs hung from the eagle's beak. She threw her head back, sucked the rest of the dog down.

The following day, Birthday began to fly.

A great shadow circled above the farm. Children walking through town shrunk in fear. Garbage cans were pulled into the heavens, emptied aluminum drums crashed down two miles away. Every stray animal, injured or slow, vanished overnight.

She was awoken by shrieking in the moonlight.

Birthday was perched on the barn. She walked outside and said, "Birthday, do you remember me? I am your mother."

Her long wing reached down and Michelle took hold of a feather. Suddenly they were ascending, the clouds nearing, the dark fields below—a mile, and then another mile, below. She took a deep breath and the algid air was remarkably thin.

"Where to?"

Her eagle cooed.

At first light, they flew over the snow-capped mountains. At lunch, they followed the twisted rivers until they broke over sharp falls. By dinner, the frantic mess of the silver city was spilling below. She noticed a train pulling into the station, and realized she'd forgotten her parents at the station.

"Shit! We've got to land."

Birthday responded, gliding towards the waiting platform. They came in hot, talons out, catching the metal railing. The train conductor yanked wildly on the brake. Over the P.A. system, he yelled, "Dragon!"

Michelle's father opened his window, "Michelle! What are you doing?"

"I'm here to pick you up."

"Oh god," Mom said in disgust. "Let me guess, that's the contents of your beloved egg?"

Michelle opened her mouth to speak, but before she could, Birthday lunged against the train and pulled mom out, crunching down on her head.

On they flew. Onward and onward. She washed the blood and mud and ash off Birthday with a hose. They were in a motel parking lot, just outside Cheyenne. The clerk was peeking out the window, his head just below the neon sign reading No Vacancy, and she pleaded, "We just need a minute, please don't—" The curtains closed and she knew he was on the phone. No one really wants to help you in this life. When Michelle heard police sirens, both she and Birthday knew there would be no rest for them, no peace, they knew to leave society. They slept on a higher cliff, overlooking an eternity of rocky debris; the debris changing color through the day, pink with the dawn, and yellowing in the midmorning, and then in the white light of midday, the debris looked like chalk broke off, fallen here; as the day ended, the trash, the debris, the waste, took on a purple hue as night slipped over everything like an uncontrollable power. It was boring and Michelle was talking to Birthday like the bird was her therapist. She felt overcome by a numbness she pitied other animals couldn't feel, couldn't appreciate. They flew on, directionless because much of the world looks roughly the same—beautiful stuff that you get used to in just five short minutes of admiring it.

She didn't guide Birthday, and Birthday seemed to have no plan, either. The universe showed its random, chaotic face. But then Michelle broke out of her trance staring into the endless nothing of rolling clouds, down below, hundreds of feet was a twisting road snaking through the mountain. A man on a red motorcycle, the patch on the back of the jacket a golden viper; the helmet of the rider unmistakably identified the person. Birthday swooped down. The man on the motorcycle must have felt like a mouse. He looked back over his shoulder and saw the giant eagle, and he must have screamed—he lost control of the motorcycle and off the edge of the mountain he went, riding it down like Evel Knievel. For over a hundred feet the rider and the bike fell, fell, fell like a stone. Just before they struck a crag of steely granite, Birthday caught the motorcycle in one claw, and the rider in the other. They landed on the floor of the canyon, a wind ripping through the mountain pass.

Michelle jumped off the bird's back and walked to the rider, who was lying flat on his back. Shocked. Arms out in an X. His boots were trembling as his legs shook. She kneeled down and looked at herself reflected in the mirrored face of the helmet's visor. Her figure looked distorted and wild; that's how she felt, so that was fine, was suiting. She flipped open the visor and looked at the man's face. "Eric," she said. He was quiet, but making a sound like he was choking on the words. "Michelle," he finally croaked out, and looking up at Birthday, he rolled over and puked into the dust.

In a minute he was sitting up, and having yanked the helmet off his head, he was no longer breathing as hard. His eyes went from Michelle to Birthday and back, over and over again. No one was speaking. "What is this?" Eric said.

"What's what?" She pointed at Birthday, big as a house, looming over her shoulder. "This is my friend. She's cool." Michelle turned and rubbed Birthday's feathers. She said, "You're so cool, Birthday, aren't you? You aren't going to eat Eric, you're so cool."

Birthday lunged forward and snapped her beak on the rear tire of the motorcycle and then she soared off into the valley, leaving Michelle and Eric some privacy to talk.

"What is this, some kid of revenge?"

"This wasn't even my idea," Michelle said. "I'm just along for the ride."

"Where did you find it … the bird."

"She found me."

"Well that's nice. I'm sorry."

"For what?"

"That we didn't work out. I regret how I acted."

"It didn't work out, big deal. You hurt me though. You disappeared. You ditched me. It worked out fine, though," Michelle said.

"Do you want to talk about things?"

"We're talking. And no."

"I didn't mean to abandon you."

"You're just worried you're gonna get eaten."

"I didn't mean to ..." he stammered.

"Ah, everything is beyond everyone's control. What a fun existence. Oh my God ..." Michelle turned to look, Birthday was flying back into the mountain pass. She barely fit now, coming in for a rough landing, shrieking in Eric's face.

"Birthday!" Michelle yelled, trying to hold back her laughter.

The motorcycle was gone. The motorcycle was never seen again. When he asked about the motorcycle, she said, "I think Birthday is fucking with you."

Night fell. Michelle and Eric climbed back on Birthday and they flew over the darkened canyons. And they slept as Birthday flew them farther through the night. When Michelle opened her eyes, the sun was just coming up over the desert. Eric said, "Can you take me back to where I was?"

She said, "I think you're coming along."

"I don't want to come along."

Michelle slapped Birthday's neck, and she glided down to the desert floor. Death Valley some people call it. Eric jumped off and stumbled away from them. He said, "Well, it was good seeing you again, Mellissa!"

"My name is Michelle."

"It was so good seeing you, Michelle."

He walked away.

She yelled, "You'll die here! Come with me!"

He said, "It was good seeing you again, Michelle!"

Birthday beat her wings, sand blasted Eric. She took to the sky. Dawn came quicker, just the two of them.

After that Birthday flew north, towards the mountains at the tippy top of America. She ripped goats from the peaks, and Michelle cooked them at the fire, saying, "Guess I'm starving enough to no longer be a vegetarian."

Michelle felt like one often does in exodus. Birthday wrapped her in her wings and they slept, nestled at the edge of a cave. A bear moaned down below, and it sounded like breakfast.

She called Dad from a ski slope pay phone.

"Where are you, girl?"

"I just touch-downed out of the clouds to tell you, I'm sorry."

"Sorry?" he said. "You can't really be sorry, can you? I don't hear it in your voice. I don't hear anything in your voice. I just hear me me me me me me me me me me."

"You're drunk, I can tell."

"So? So I'm drunk? I'm grieving the loss of two women I used to love. I'm on my way, you know. To get you," he said. "Stay where you are."

"Please just let me be. Please. Let us be. It's for your own good."

"No chance."

The line went dead.

Their new life at the top of the world. Their new life swinging into tropical jungles. Life on Birthday's back, talons extended, extracting sleeping lions from the swaying grass. In the tallest tree, they made a nest. The wavering heat of the day. The sky forever. Michelle threw her furs into the river, carried a rhino tusk, sweat every second. Her hair was one tangled dreadlock that she fantasized about shaving down to the scalp. She longed for paperback books and music other than Birthday's shrieks. Or she longed to forget the human language entirely and revert back into prehistory.

When the helicopter came across the jungle, it was obvious, yet she said, wishfully, "That's not for us, Birthday. They're not coming for us."

"Michelle!" her father shouted through the speakers. It was his helicopter. She began to hyperventilate. Birthday's eyes met her own and she felt strong again—could breathe. She waved her father off. "Go away! Leave us alone!" She watched him through the glass, he put the microphone to his mouth and spoke, his amplified voice sounding like a monster, torn to shreds. "Give up!" She flipped him off. Machine gun fire pierced the jungle air, tut tut tut tut tut. A rattle of doom. Michelle ducked down and screamed; tut tut tut tut tut, bullets ripping into the giant eagle, who didn't seem to notice, or care—tut tut tut tut tut.

The nose of the whirly bird dipped. Birthday beat her wings. The machine gun fire paused. Michelle though, Good, you've figured out it's useless. A missile soared towards them. For a second, Michelle wondered what Hell would feel like when it kissed her. But as the missile got closer, Birthday opened her beak and swallowed it. Nothing happened. No ill effect. The helicopter wobbled in the sky, and then attempted to bank out of the way in retreat. But it was too late, Birthday was already in pursuit of her easy prey, calling out an attack cry. Wings whipping. Talons out.

The Moon

WE MET AT A PLANETARIUM. I WAS ON PAROLE AND getting blood tests every month. I'd started doing LSD as often as possible because it didn't show up on their tests, and I still needed to live on a different world.

The sidewalk splitting apart, I walked two miles in the rain to attend the laser light show. When I got there, I found out I was mistaken, like I often am. I paid the six dollars to the ticket taker, and went in and looked at fake versions of the real stars projected on a big domed black nothing.

There was only one other person in the amphitheater. I was tripping so hard, I sat down right next to her and leaned over and said, "Where's the lasers?" She said, "You're soaking wet." I took off my shirt and she howled with joy.

After the show we went out to her white Mustang and screwed on the hood of the car. Nobody cared about us. Then we sat in the car for hours, just talking, mostly talking about how nobody on Earth cared about us, a popular topic. The engine was off. The windows fogging up. I could see and feel the world disappearing. Jane said she had simply replaced a vodka problem with fucking, the same way that some people replace the whatever ails ya with Jesus. Or with tennis. Or with suicide. She said it was a shame she had met me now, she felt a real connection to me, and would like to be exclusive, and in love or something like it. She said it was sad.

"Sad why?"

"Oh, sad because I'm leaving."

I had a job at a medieval themed gas station. Nobody else would hire me. I had to wear a plastic suit of armor. Two days after our initial meeting at the planetarium, Jane pulled up to the pump and I filled her tank, but I had my visor down, she didn't know it was me. She was so kind to this stranger in the suit of plastic armor. I'd never met a kinder, gentler person. I decided then that I would do anything with her, that I would go anywhere with her, long as I had a chance. I called from the payphone on my break, I told her that. We were together that night, and most nights after that for a while.

Before our date that night I had group therapy in the basement of the Lutheran church. The sleepy-eyed counselor had a watermelon. When the watermelon was passed to you you were supposed to speak about your feelings. He said the watermelon was like a big egg and inside the big egg was either a monster or an angel. You'd get into big trouble if you smashed the watermelon, so nobody did that. We talked when we had the watermelon and we were obligated to go into greater detail than we had when we'd held the grapefruit, when we'd held the apple before that, when we'd held a single grape and just said our name. Here's what I learned, overall—everyone just wants what they want but it's all ambiguous, even to them, no one really knows what they want, they just long for it, and it is invisible and takes no form.

Jane met me at the shooting range. I thought I saw my parole officer at the soda machine but it turned out to just be a cardboard cutout of Charleston Heston. We peeled off all our bullets and then we had sex again on the hood of her car. Still, nobody cared about us. Afterwards, engine off, windows fogged up, she asked me what my Narcotics Anonymous meetings were like. I told her, "If I tell you I'll have to lobotomize you." She said that'd be alright. She wanted to stop feeling guilty anyway. She told me her AA meetings were very helpful up to the point they became biblical, but the thing that made it hard to not get drunk was that everywhere you looked there was some subconscious advertisement for liquor. Busses passing by in the shape of wine bottles. She said, "Earth is not the kind of place to get sober." I held her hand, and told her that my meetings took place in an abandoned funhouse and that one of the guys was a speed freak who thought he was a werewolf, so whenever we were anywhere close to a full moon he didn't come in. It was for our safety. He didn't want to full moon kill us all. The counselor said, everybody here is a werewolf, okay? Everyone is cursed, is infected, has supernatural powers, knows what it is like to live between worlds.

They took my blood. I pissed in a test cup. The nurse snipped a lock of my hair with a pair of rusty scissors. My eyes were dilated and she said, "I shouldn't even be letting you take this test, your eyes are as big as the big bad wolf's."

I said, "If you want me to pop one of my eyeballs out for you to test, I'll do that."

She said, "That's not necessary. There's no eyeball analysis."

I got into trouble because I collapsed, foaming at the mouth, gun in pocket, in a playground with a rubber castle, was found there. My counseling had started out with the grape, like I said, then it was cherries. When you had the cherry in your hand you could speak about your substance(s). When we got a little better and were able to talk about bigger things, the cherry became an apple, and the apple was our regrets, our sins, so to speak. And then a grapefruit. By the time winter was over you could speak when the cantaloupe was in your hands, and you could blab on forever when you had the cantaloupe, you were almost proud. I got real into things. I grew my beard out and started braiding it. Started microdosing with psilocybin. The gas station job encouraged we look the part. I've done a lot of things I'm not proud of. I've been better. I've been worse. I've thrown a couple pineapples at the wall.

Two junkies robbed the gas station. One had a knife. The other had a sawed-off shotgun. Which was funny, because all us worker bees had plastic swords. Plastic shields. Plastic war hammers. They made off with twelve hundred dollars. Two junkies, who died later that week. I used to know them both. Very well. A past life. An original design of the gas station included a metal dragon perched on top of the snack shop that would belch fire up into the sky so cars streaming by on the highway would see the spectacle and be compelled to take the offramp and investigate. In my experience, no one really knows what they are doing. Even the fire marshal.

Jane wanted to go camping, just the two of us, up in the mountains. I skipped my watermelon meeting in the basement of the Lutheran church. I drove to her house in my pickup. Her Mustang wasn't in the driveway.

She came out her door with a sleeping bag under her arm. She kissed my lips deeply, my head hanging out the window.

"Where's your Mustang?"

"Sold it."

"You sold it? I don't believe it."

"I ride my bicycle to work now. It's for the best, more exercise, you'll like the results, haha."

We went narrowly across state lines and I got a boner. I was breaking parole! The mountains. Ascension into the sky! We climbed out of the car. Jane got naked in the moonlight. My eyes were wide, studying the pale skin reflecting the moon back at itself and making her appear otherworldly.

"Forget that car, the bicycle is a good thing."

"I thought you'd say that."

We laid down on our sides in the soft grass and felt around for the switches on each other's bodies that would reveal all of the mysteries of light and horror, patience, doubt, desire and truth.

After we worked up a good sweat, we walked hand in hand down to the lake below and washed the sweat off. We swam out into the dark water with the stars and the moon shining down onto us, making everything shimmer.

That night, we slept in the bed of the truck, flat on our backs. Jane kept staring up at the sky, as if she was seeing it for the first time. She'd blink slowly, her eyelashes trailing behind her lids.

"I've always felt close to the moon."

"Yeah?"

"When I was a little girl, I had a dream every night about walking around on the moon. Living there. Having a life. Look at all of that light. Imagine being in the middle of that glowing?"

"It'd be nice, I suppose."

"To live in a dream."

"I want to leave, too," I said.

"You should," she said. "Where do you want to go?"

"I want to go down to South America and find the Ibioga tree."

"What's up with the Ibioga tree?"

"Gets you fucked up."

"Ah—maybe you'd be better off on a world where you couldn't get fucked up."

"I'd rather die."

My parole officer said, "Get the fuck out of here, I don't want to see you like this again. This is an insult!"

There was a for sale sign on her front lawn beneath the dying elm tree.

My heart fell sharply and broke another one of my ribs. My heart is a wrecking ball. Don't you have one like me? Doesn't yours swing wildly when given cause and create all kinds of internal damage?

"You're really going away," I said. She nodded. I said, "Still?"

"How many times and in how many ways do I have to tell you?" I wanted to see Jane that weekend but she said she was busy. When I pushed the request, she got quiet and evasive.

"I have plans."

"Alright."

The way Jane handled it, how she anxiously changed the subject, fidgety and awkward, I figured I was probably 'the other guy'. Jane was important to me. Already my heart was like a stone falling and chipping the inside of my ribcage. She had a secret. I could tell that she was balancing me against the secret, seeing which would stick and which she would have to give up.

So, headlights off, I tailed her. She cruised ahead on her bicycle. Oblivious. Head in the clouds. I put my truck in neutral and coasted downhill through the sleeping town.

It surprised me when Jane took a turn down a quiet road, just past the abandoned Wicker World plaza, that I knew from experience led nowhere. She glided into a farther abandoned strip mall with a bowling alley and a Food Universe that'd been closed for some time.

But, there were other cars in the potholed lot.

I watched Jane lean her bicycle against the wall of the bowling alley. A beacon of light washed over her as she entered the door. The light snuffed out as the door closed on its own.

I parked, and crept in behind her.

There was a group of people sitting in the bowling alley, having some strange meeting. A bald man with small spectacles that made him look like a mole, stood in front of the crowd. He wore a button up white dress shirt and had a lot of pens in his breast pocket. The pens made me think he was important for some reason. Through the crack of the door, I tried to listen but they were speaking too low. I watched the backs of their heads for a while, specifically, the back of Jane's head. Periodically I'd note that she would enthusiastically nod her head. What was she nodding about? A few minutes later, I saw her rise and ask a question. It nearly drove me insane not knowing what the question was. I should have crept closer, perhaps crawling on my belly like a boy playing soldier, infiltrating the enemy line—instead, I got nervous and left.

She was at my window late that night, pebbles bouncing off the glass. "You awake?"

"I am."

"Let me in."

I opened the window and she climbed into my room. Her body was warm and her neck was salty. "Do you still go to your AA meetings?"

"No. I told you. Too biblical."

"Okay, I thought you said that."

That weekend, again, she was too busy to see me. I couldn't figure her out. Hot. Then cold. I stumbled into her neighbor's undulating rainbow wonderland yard. Then I saw she was having a yard sale. She was selling everything she owned. I hid behind the trash cans and watched for what could have been ten minutes or ten hours. Soon she was alone and surrounded by dishes and cups and jackets and vinyl records and Ikea furniture. I crossed the street.

"I followed you, once."

"What?"

"To the old bowling alley on Mill Road," I said.

"Oh."

She admitted, "I was worried about this conversation."

"What were you doing there?"

"If I told you, you'd think I was nuts."

"Try me."

"Okay. Come in the house."

We left all the things out there on the lawn, unattended. She shut the front door and looked out the bay window. No one was coming anyway.

"Just say it quick, like pulling a band aid off. Zip. It won't hurt as much."

She turned to look at me.

"I belong to a sect and we worship the moon, I don't know how to put it any other way."

"A moon cult?"

"Ha! A moon cult! No, I don't think I'd call it a moon cult, it's not that at all ... well, uhhhh, maybe it is kinda a moon cult."

"Alright."

She'd sold her Mustang, gave them the money. Her house was just about to close with a realtor. She was giving the money to them too.

"For what?"

"We're going to the moon."

"You're gonna fly a spaceship to the moon?"

"Not exactly. Come with me."

"I couldn't."

"I want you to."

She was brainwashed. There was no way of talking any sense into her about it. I knew what I had to do. It was simple, I just had to go with her to her next meeting and grab that mole-faced man with all the pens and get him to—to what?

I'd just shake the living hell out of him. If that didn't work, I'd start punching. That always seems to help.

I drove Jane up into those same mountains. There was a large structure there now. A bridge that went up above the pine trees a hundred feet, stopping at the mouth of the night sky.

"Thanks for the ride," she said. "I wish that you'd change your mind, come with me."

The people were all standing around in a cluster, looking up at the sky. As we got nearer, I noticed the serious man with all the pens consulting a chart of stars. He'd look at the map and then look at the tree-line, back to the map and then up at the full moon.

"Yup, tonight's our night."

There was excitement in the air, as if those were people waiting on the dock for a cruise ship that would take them on a voyage around the tropics. They smiled, standing tall with their suitcases, all silently wondering, "Do I have all I'll need for the moon?"

I was about to go over and start shaking the mole man until all his pens fell out of his pocket.

But, as predicted, the moon appeared to be getting bigger and bigger. Swelling up. Getting closer and closer. The people went like this, "Oooooow!"

"Ahhhhhh!"

"It's coming!"

A few of the more eager ones began to clap and jump up and down. Jane grabbed onto me so hard that her fingernails went into my forearm and nearly raised blood. I didn't notice. I was staring up at the sky. The moon swelled and swelled and a light came over us, so white and blinding that it was hard to keep my eyes open. I had to peek through the bottom of my eyelids.

Like an orange hanging from a tree, the moon was then immediately over us. Some of the people went up the structure and simply stepped onto the moon.

"I'm going," she said. "But, you should come."

"Where?"

"Up into the sky and then space. Who knows after that?"

"I'm not sure."

She took my hand and we went up the structure. She led me like a child walking with a balloon.

"Don't be scared," she pleaded. I let go of her hand. She stepped onto the moon, and I stood there on the platform, having made my decision.

"Jump!"

"I can't."

"You can."

"I love you."

I thought about it for a minute. I finally said. "Have a great time up there."

"Last chance!" she yelled, pain in her voice.

I shook my head and the mole man pulled her back into the bright light. She took her place with all the others. They looked so happy. What a blissful moment for them. Jane looked like she was crying. Or it was just too bright for her eyes. No, she was definitely crying. I waved goodbye. She covered her face. What a kind and gentle sweetheart. The moon started going up and up and up. Jane got smaller, and the moon got smaller too. It got smaller until it was just a speck up there in the sky, looking farther away than normal. And I was all alone on the platform. But this was also the day that I was finally off parole. I didn't have to pump gas anymore in a suit of plastic armor. Wooooo. What a relief.

When the police took my driver's license away from me, I began to ride Jane's bicycle. The exercise felt good. And watermelons were just watermelons again.

rek-rek-kek-kek-kek

BELOW MY WINDOW, I HEARD THE SAD GRIND OF someone trying to start their car: rek-rek-kek-kek-kek; rek-rek-kek-kek-kek; rek-rek-kek-kek-kek.

I got excited, and then felt bad. And then came the howling of the fire engine moving up John F. Kennedy Blvd. But still underneath that: rek-rek-kek-kek-kek; rek-rek-kek-kek-kek; rek-rek-kek-kek-kek.

Rek-rek-kek-kek-kek; rek-rek-kek-kek-kek. The driver got out, a faceless nobody, who could have passed as my doppelgänger. A quick glance under the hood, a shrug, the driver returned to the wheel. Rek-rek-kek-kek-kek; rek-rek-kek-kek-kek.

Finally the engine caught. The wraithlike screech of the fan belt: eeeeeeeeeeeeee! But the engine died again flllrrrbbrbb. A hissing. I would have quit then.

More determined Rek-rek-kek-kek-kek; rek-rek-kek-kek-kek, rek-rek-kek-kek-kek, rek-rek-kek-kek-kekrek-rek-kek-kek-kek!

Even more determined Rek-rek-kek-kek-kekrek-rek-kekkek-kekrek-rek-kek-kek-kekrek-rek-kek-kek-kekrek-rek-kek-kek-kekrek-rek-kek-kek-kek!!

But this time the engine caught, and held! And the driver screamed in triumph! And the fan belt screamed in triumph, eeeeeeeeeeee! I jumped up and down in celebration too, the venetian blinds waved wildly. The driver gunned the rusted car up the street, turned left on a red light, left their birthplace—this predictable, dreamless east.

40 hours later the driver arrived at the Pacific Ocean, jumped out of the car and went to the bathroom off the side of the cliff. Relieved, and feeling like they had gained some previously unavailable power, they stood, hands on hips, overlooking the ocean. To no one, not to God, the driver said, "Dope luv it."

And here's what the car sounded like in the west after it stalled out on the cliff: Rek-rek-kek-kek-kekrek-rek-kek-kek-kek.

And here's what the car sounded like as it was pushed off the cliff into the surging surf below: Ba-boooooosssssh!

And the driver walked along the road as the sun set. It was time to snake blindly farther ahead. They walked all through the night, thinking, planning, encountering nothing but the pin prick pain of the past. In the morning they bought a blue Datsun from a used car dealership, drove headlong towards the source of that remembered pain.

The Datsun got them down through Mexico, Guatemala, Honduras, Nicaragua, finally Costa Rica where it went: rek-rek-kek-kek-kekrek-rek-kek-kek-kek.

And the rain came down and the blue Datsun sunk in the mud, rek-rek-kek-kek-kek.

It sank until it was obscured in the wet ooze of the earth, the driver still at the wheel. A sloth heard the muffled groan of the car beneath the mud. The car went: rek-rek-kek-kek-kek. The sloth smiled the slow way sloths do.

But the rain stopped! And the mud dried! And the next day the driver dug out of their grave and ran, caked in dirt, into Columbia.

Having washed off in a waterfall, and having found a restful town, the driver put their feet up. A man dressed in white, tipped his hat and brought a cup of fine steaming coffee. "¿A dónde vas amigo?"

The driver answered, "I should have thought of this, I don't speak your language." The man in white said, "El camino es largo para los perdidos."

And wow this Columbian sunshine! So much more desirable than Jersey City, New Jersey.

The driver continued on burro into South America, slicing through vines with a small sword; the travel was merciless, offering no reward. The burro laid down and died. The driver poked the burro, but the burro remained in its final state. And through the hot nights, terrible dreams of failure came to the driver: rek-rek-kek-kek-kekrek-rek-kek-kek-kek.

Venezuela. The driver woke up with a pink boa constrictor wrapped around them. French Guyana. Chased by a tiger across a raging river, the driver ducked and leapt and outsmarted and redirected death, away, away. Brazil. Scaling a green mountain, the driver looked down on an infinite wall of green jungle, and then descended that green mountain, began to cut through vast green jungle with the small sword, entering into the bluff of infinity with a heart aimed at a seemingly lost cause. Out of sight, and out of contact, who knows what happens to the source of our pain?

Sunburnt, exhausted, near-death, the driver finally stood on the shore of the Southern Atlantic Ocean. Rio De Janeiro. Paradise. The driver looked up at the giant statue of Christ the Redeemer with his arms flung wide, looming on the tallest peak. The driver closed their eyes, believing the journey of life to be pointless. The driver's mind went: rek-rek-kek-kek-kek, rek-rek-kek-kek-kek.

But then a sweet voice called from over their shoulder. "I thought you'd never come." The driver turned and looked at the face of their estranged lover. "Came here to say you're an asshole, and I'm an asshole, too."

They embraced! Swelling music! Kisses and promises! I'll do better, what was I thinking??? Romance in Rio De Janeiro! A new beginning and the wounds of yesterday drowned in the shining sea, buried alive on the sands of Copocabana Beach, taken on a lovely visit to the Museum of Tomorrow.

Tomorrow, I like the sound of that. The possibility of that. A lot of people don't even know that word. Tomorrow. Tomorrow in ny language means the same thing.

And then three weeks later the redefined lovebirds sucked up their fear of jet airplanes and flew back here, to this gloomy, nothing-doing, gray gray block. They got married at the courthouse on Montgomery Ave. over by the sandwich shop and the karate dojo, and then they moved into the apartment above me. I began to hear them walking around sometimes. Such heavy shoes. I began to wonder.

One morning I finally saw them together in the foyer of the building. The driver was adding the lover's name to the PO box. I officially introduced myself. The driver no longer looked anything like me. They each shook my hand, feigning enthusiasm. I got my mail. It was all worthless junk. I said, "We should hang out sometime. Celebrate your joy." They smiled. Together, they were so beautiful. I couldn't believe they'd come back here.

Two days later I looked out the widow and there was a new rusted car in the spot where the old rusted car used to be. Both of them were in it—mad. Yelling. The car wouldn't start. It went: rek-rek-kek-kek-kek; rek-rek-kek-kek-kek.

And then: rek-rek-kek-kek-kek; rek-rek-kek-kek-kek; rek-rek-kek-kek-kek; rek-rek-kek-kek-kek; rek-rek-kek-kek-kek.

More determined rek-rek-kek-kek-kekrek-rek-kek-kekkekrek-rek-kek-kek-kekrek-rek-kek-kek-kekrek-rek-kek-kek-kek.

The lover climbed out of the passenger side and walked away. The wind whipped down Kennedy Blvd. The driver jumped out, abandoning the car, leaving the door hanging open. Shouldering the wind, they followed in pursuit. "Wait." The lover looked back, held out a hand. They hustled off, together. Then I heard the fire engines howling. And then the relative quiet of everything else, after. My fingers slipped from the blind.

I called the liquor store when it opened for the day, and ordered two bottles of their bubbliest but not most expensive champagne. The clerk said, "The bubbliest is the most expensive."

On three separate minor expeditions, I went upstairs, knocking loud on their mauve door, but they weren't home, or not answering. Later, I drank the champagne, alone, in my apartment, watching out the window, staring at their rusted car for what felt like more than a lifetime.

Random Balloons

SOMEONE WAS JACKHAMMERING OUTSIDE THE window. I rolled over, separated the venetian blinds, looked outside. A gray haired woman in a high visibility vest. Excavating. I watched for a while. She was all alone. Cars just driving around her. A mother walked by on the other sidewalk holding the hands of two tiny children. No acknowledgement. The woman with the jackhammer made a serious face, braced her body and pulled the trigger. She shook violently. Hair flying around. The street broke apart.

I microwaved old coffee. The apartment was like a snow globe but the snow was suspended dust and fuzz, floating. Life was a gel. Was an ooze. I drank the coffee by the window watching the jackhammering, wishing this was a professional sporting event so I could learn more about the athlete busting the roadway apart. Her adversities. Her setbacks. Her small triumphs that led her here. What was on the line. Something was wrong with the street, that is all I knew. She was here to fix it, all alone. I set the coffee on the dresser. Sometimes I jackhammer at work. For some reason I'm not at work.

My phone rang. The front door was connected to my phone. When people enter 001 into the keypad it calls my phone because I am the first apartment. The buzzer is complicated. The system is complicated. The world is complicated. Death is complicated. I answered the phone.

A voice like a frog croaked, "Pizza."

I replied to the voice, "I didn't order a pizza." I checked the clock, it was 9:15am. But this wasn't the pizza man.

"Just buzz me in," the frog said, "I got Chinese food or something."

I hung up the phone. It might be someone entering the building with a sawed-off shot gun. They might be here to blast everyone in the stomach with the shotgun. It was Wednesday, five days before New Years, what better time? Immediately my phone rang, I answered. "Pizza," the frog said again. I buzzed the shotgun frog in. I admired their tenacity. I admire everyone's tenacity.

Yesterday I read a work of profound classic literature. The book changed my life. Immediately after finishing the book I went online and read all the one star reviews that people gave the book. The best review was by a guy who was very upset he couldn't get his money back after he finished the book. The review mentioned that he had contacted the used bookstore in Virginia and the bookstore owner was like, "I'm not giving you your two bucks back." The reviewer said he couldn't wait until he was dead so he could see that author in the afterlife and whoop their ass over the two bucks. After clicking another magic button I was able to see all the other reviews the person had done; three stars for a pair of children's mirrored rainbow sunglasses; five stars for an ordinary incandescent lightbulb; five stars for neon gravel, the kind you would put in a fish tank; one star for a Phillip's head screwdriver. When I clicked on the review of the Phillip's head screwdriver, it was a rant about how he didn't see why the world was so absurd and why everyone couldn't just get on board together to make existing easier. Only he said it like this—I needed flat head! Fail! Ahh! You had one job!

The jackhammering stopped. I heard voices. The police were here. The police were talking to the woman with the jackhammer. Turns out there was nothing wrong with the street. Cool. She nonchalantly took off her high visibility vest and threw it into the bed of a pickup truck parked right in front of my car. God, I always forget where I've parked. It's always a surprise. Angry, she flung the hefty jackhammer into the bed of the truck. Then greater silence, the air compressor shut off. I was intrigued. The woman was yelling now. Hands thrown in the air. She was yelling at the police with her hands. Both cops took a step back and I was like—Damn! I'm about to see American gun violence! I raised the blinds. I opened the window. I was right there, six feet over the action. I had VIP seats. A third cop car swooped in, coming the wrong way down the one way street. In under a minute the woman was in handcuffs and in the back of one of the police cars. And the cops were lingering. They lingered for a while. They lingered—mad—glaring at the hole in the road. Then they saw me in the window, leaning out with my coffee. "Did you see this?" I shook my head. I said, "I didn't see nothing." They all had shaved heads and wrap around rainbow sunglasses. Three stars. I said, "I didn't see nothing." The shortest cop was especially mad. "Oh? Yeah? You didn't see nothing, huh? Hanging out the window like the town gossip and you didn't see anything?" I said, "I'm blind. Who am I talking to? Charlie is that you? Charlie?" The cops left with the woman. And the morning was cold and totally blank. It wasn't even 10am.

I opened the top dresser drawer and ate the rest of the mushrooms that my wife had claimed had 'gone bad', whatever that could mean. Washed them down with warm tap water. Got dressed. Finally found my shoes. Walked out into the world.

There were two flyers stuck to not only our apartment door, but every apartment door in the building. One flyer was from Goldie's Fried Chicken, they wanted to sell us chickens. They wanted this entire building to band together and help rid the world of its greatest scourge, the chicken. We were all to do our part by consuming this animal. The other flyer was from the building itself. The building was sentient. The building was holding a meeting down in its guts on Tuesday. We were all invited to attend and cast our vote for banning smoking from every single apartment and from also, the area right outside the apartment. Secondhand smoke was giving everyone cancer. This apartment building was transforming into a hospital, or a gulag. If you didn't come to the meeting Tuesday night at 7pm, that also meant that by default you were voting in favor of banning smoking. I ripped the flyer to shreds and stomped on it. I had never smoked a cigarette in my life but here I was with a mission! I was headed out to the Uzbek deli to buy a hundred dollars worth of cigarettes and I was going to smoke them ALL in my apartment—today.

Outside the building, Joe the smoker was smoking where he

usually smoked.

"They're trying to ban smoking!" I said. "I can't believe it."

He said, "Trying? Vote was last night. They banned it."

"That Tuesday?" I said in disbelief. "Not this Tuesday?"

"What?"

"What?"

"You heard me," he said, spitting.

I looked at Joe. What a law breaking badass.

He had piss yellow long hair. A gray van dyke goatee. A Batman baseball cap. A jean jacket. He was smoking a strawberry cigarillo.

"Wait, I really missed the vote?"

"You really missed the vote. Where were you?"

"I was home finishing this amazing book. A profound work of classic literature that this guy on the internet gave one star to, and then I got sucked into reading all his other reviews. Was kind of incredible really. He gave a wheelbarrow two stars. He gave an egg timer five stars and said if he could he would have given it six. He gave a can of Pledge two stars."

"What's an egg timer for?"

"Exactly, Joe!"

He was done with his cigar so he went back into the building without saying goodbye. I walked around the side and took a good look at the new hole in the road. It served no logical purpose. Someone had just decided to destroy the road. My car had a bunch of dust all over it. I stared at the dust for awhile. Then I looked in the back of the pickup truck. The air compressor and the jackhammer were still there. The police had left them there. I would have thought they would have liked to use it all as evidence. Thought maybe the judge would like to see. I don't know. I guess if you just start destroying the road, the judge is just like: Hey whatever, I don't need to see anything. You've committed the gravest offense. You have gone out of your way to destroy society. You are making everything harder for everyone. You are creating an impasse. You are an impasse. And now our society shall destroy ye.

I found a rag in the back of the pickup. I took it out and wiped down my car. And then I stunk like diesel fuel because the rag had been used to clean up the diesel fuel that spilled out of the air compressor. And now my car was covered in a fine layer of diesel. It was all starting to make sense! I looked up into my window and watched my own ceiling fan for awhile. It was so cold out here. But the ceiling fan was always on in the apartment because the radiators were always singing singing singing. In the window above my own, I saw a hand with a cigarette. I shouted up at the hand, "YOU THERE ON THE SECOND FLOOR! YOU'RE UNDER ARREST." From my vantage, the hand disappeared. I crossed the street to get a better look up at the window. I watched the drapes draw closed.

I walked down the street. I couldn't figure out if I had a job anymore or if I was on vacation. I checked my pockets for evidence that I still had a job. Hm, some money. Not a lot of money. Just some money. The amount of money a person would have if they had just recently lost their job. But maybe I had more money in the bank? I checked my wallet. Hmm, a debit card. I walked over to the Uzbek deli. I put my card in the ATM machine. My balance said I was neither rich nor poor. I had the exact average amount of money I always had. I let out a disgusted sigh. The deli man said, "You okay?" I nodded. I said, "I can't figure out if I have a job anymore." He said, "I heard that they are hiring over there at the ninety nine cent store." I said, "Oh, that's incredible." He said, "Yeah, you have a diploma? High school at least? GED?" I said, "How much could they possibly pay at the ninety nine cent store?" He grinned, "Ninety nine cents an hour, haha, I don't know."

My phone buzzed. It was the group text for the guys I worked(?) with at the chemical plant. Someone had had a baby. Someone's someone had had a baby. Congratulations! I bought a bunch of cigarettes and a giant blunt, the kind you're supposed to rip apart and fill with weed, well, I just bought it to celebrate the birth of the baby. Outside the store, shivering in the cold, snot leaking out of my nose, I looked at my phone, at the anonymous pink baby being nuzzled by someone and I tried to figure out who it was. Who anyone was. I texted: Do I still work with you guys? Right away there was a text: hahaha if you call it that. Another: fuk u. Another: unfortunately but we can dream. I walked back into the Uzbek deli and I told the guy I still had a job. Thanks for the lead. He looked happy for me. Did a little clap. I walked down the block to the ninety nine cent store. I went inside. I was so overjoyed and relieved I was almost weeping. I wouldn't have to work there after all. One giant display was just all kinds of random balloons. Like all the world wanted was balloons. I held my hands up in triumph. I wouldn't have to work retail, selling balloons and macaroni and cheese and squirt guns to just make ninety nine cents an hour. I could afford to eat Goldie's Chicken every meal until it gave me a cardiac arrest. Another text: u still on vacation? I texted back: maybe.

When I got home the people from the township were there filling in the hole. Loud fat guys having fun. Orange sweatshirts. Big gloves. Dumping bags of asphalt into the hole. Making the problem disappear. They were the repairmen of the entire universe. Some maniac comes around and makes something more difficult, more dangerous, you just call these guys and they come and it all works out. Great noble beasts summoned from their sacred caves. Working together. Oh, yo, let me get that for you. A knife slicing the bag open, the asphalt sliding down, plooooop. They were ignoring me as I stared at them, to a point. Then I said, "I saw the whole thing. This lady just started going wacko. Making all this racket. Destroying society."

Surprised at first, and then grinning, one guy said, "Bro, I know."

"We heard, we heard," the other guy said. He had a hand tamper he was compacting the road patch with.

I pointed at her truck. Michigan license plates. I pointed in the bed of the pickup truck. We all looked at the jackhammer and the air compressor.

One of the guys said, "You gonna drive all the way from fucking Michigan to this place just to crunch it all up. Whacked."

"Whacked," the other guy said.

"Whacked," I said.

I tried the doors but they were locked. I peeked in the windows but couldn't see any other evidence about the life of this misunderstood woman. That's what she was. Misunderstood. If only we could understand her better. I decided to visit her in jail. I'd get to know her. I'd come forward. I'd be the star witness in her defense. I'd take the stand. Those shaved head cops would be there, having just given their testimonies against this strange woman and under cross examination I would contest them! I'd say confidently, actually I am not blind. I'd seen it all. I'd seen the entire incident. This woman was not only misunderstood, she was also innocent! I am not blind you fucking idiots!

Before the repairmen of the universe left, I urged them to take the air compressor. Urged them to take the jackhammer. They said, nah nah, we good. We good, bro. We ain't thieves, bro. But you good, we didn't see nothing either, hehehe. Later, bro. They left in their orange truck. I leaned against the misunderstood Michigan truck and relaxed for a minute. My car was melting. The diesel would eat all the paint and then the next time I saw it it would just be bare metal like the Terminator after its skin gets cooked off at the end of the first movie. Also, I was parked at the fire hydrant. These things happen. I walked around to the front of the building. I took out my giant blunt. I looked at it. It was stupid and I had no way to light it. Owning a cigar company was one of the wisest business decisions. Currently there are seven billion people cluttered together on this earth. Five babies born every second. A tidal wave of people all with reason to celebrate five times a second. You can never know everyone, and never properly celebrate them, but you can die trying. True though, everybody was a brand new isolated incident, estranged from even themselves. And I didn't own a lighter. The wind got wilder. I wanted to sit down on the sidewalk and freeze to the sidewalk and be walked on for the remaining eternity of my city. The door to the building opened. Joe again. I waved. He frowned and half-heartedly waved and kept walking. "Wait! Let's smoke!" He yelled something at me that I couldn't decode. But that is what being alive is all about. Messages sent, and messages received, and hardly any of those messages making any sense at all. I watched his jean jacket get father and father away. And then the wind knocked his Batman baseball cap into traffic and I laughed like crazy. It was one of the funniest things I'd ever seen. He hustled out during a break of cars and picked up the smashed hat. On the safety of the sidewalk, he brushed it off, and then seeing the futility, he threw it back into the rushing traffic. Here have this. Screw it.

I went back inside and lit a cigarette on the gas range. And then I leaned against the counter and held the cigarette in my hand, not even puffing on it, just letting it burn down. I lit another on the gas range and held it in my other hand. I was doing it. I was smoking in my apartment. Gradually the light of day got brighter—and get this—then the light of day got dimmer dimmer dimmer dimmer. It stayed that way for a while. And then we did it all again.

American Flags

MY FAMILY ATE AMERICAN FLAGS FOR TWO YEARS. Twenty four full moons and then Mom walked back into town and got a job again. She'd bring us cans of soup. Red cabbage. Butter pickles. Dad held out longer, he kept eating American flags, saying yum. He'd still feed them to me and my brother whenever Mom left. There was a crate full of them near the edge of the ravine. Nothing could be done. We sat around the woods stinking, chewing the stars and stripes like moo cows. And we were homeschooled so Dad would point at the letter 'A' and say, "The letter A is a lie." I'd nod, because I was older and understood these things, I said, "Of course." My brother said, "Well what's the truth about the letter 'A'?" Dad would say, "Sonny, that's a personal decision. That's up to you." And then Dad would say the letter B is a lie, and the letter C is too, and so on. I don't personally know very many individuals. But that's just because they weren't raised explicitly to be so. Sonny is himself, and no one else. Beat that. I like to think I'm myself, too. Dad had this great story he used to tell before he was killed, he told us his own father had had a beautiful gold dust colored car. But this one particular fat bird kept shitting on the car. So grandpa climbed the tree and caught the bird with his bare hands.

And do you know what he did to the bird? Well, I'm not going to tell you. What you think my grandfather did with the bird will tell you more about yourself than it ever could tell you about anyone, anything, anywhere, for all time. We had a family game where we made movies with a broken camera, though we had no film, and Mom said good, we were learning the importance of impermanence; of the absurdity of life, or death, or well, fill in the blank. Sometimes wild dogs would creep into camp, but they were shaky leaf little things. I went pow pow with my toy gun and the dog just blinked, and I told the dog, this is a life gun, it doesn't kill, I just gave you thirty extra years! The next day we coincidentally had thirty inches of snow fall all at once and we had to burn six hundred flags to survive. We were lucky; we weren't cursed to live as other people. My mother saved us in the spring. She made our lives fuller. She pretended to go to work one afternoon but instead she crept to the edge of the ravine and gathered the hundreds of flags that were left and she carried them to the ridiculous river and threw them in without us knowing. Whoosh. Away they went. But the beavers knew right away. All the Old Glorys got stuck in their dam and made the river flood over and the dam was destroyed and the water surged up the banks and broke apart our camp. Our family fled to the government assistance office and got vouchers for food and housing and my brother got a scoliosis test and failed, and I got a rabies shot and laughed. Dad joined a demolition crew, arguing that if you are not comfortable with the way society structures its boons, you're more suited to smash things with a sledgehammer. Common sense. When the institutions climb inside the meager house that is your humble body, and claim your body as their property, all you have to do is show no pain, and puke them back up, send them flying. I don't know what you were like when you were a kid, but I was raised eating American flags, and it made me tough, and my dreams were fireworks, and my compromises were never with anybody else in mind, just the elements. I believe if you were to rip my guts from my body and spread them out on the street in the center of my hometown, some diviner would spy something down there in the mess of me akin to The Declaration of Independence.

2

Wolves

SOME WOLVES WERE DRIVEN FROM THE FOREST where they lived and hunted. Their forest was destroyed and made into a mall with a J. Crew and an Apple Store, so the wolves found another forest.

But before too long, that forest was torn down too, and made into a golf course. The wolves were completely out of forest. And the wolves didn't golf.

For a time, they tried to survive in the suburbs, but there was nothing the wolves liked about the suburbs. They slept in moldy tool sheds or the backs of pickup trucks. They became gnarled and thin in the suburbs. There were no jobs there either. Even Animal Control refused to hire them to hunt raccoons and possums because the wolves were not qualified. Everyone else applying had a college education.

The wolves were forced to move towards the city. Housing was even worse for them in the city, though. Their entire pack could not find an economical way to split $3200 a month for a two bedroom. And besides, no one wanted a dog bigger than a French Bulldog in any of the buildings. Each wolf was the size of fifteen French Bulldogs sewn together. They applied for public housing but were denied.

Cops tried to shoot the wolves, but the wolves were faster than the cops. The wolves darted into the subways, sprinting through the darkened tunnels. Sometimes startled by the illuminated eye of a godspeed train, they leapt over electrified rails onto tiled platforms, and bounded up new staircases, to a different block, only to repeat it all again. More cops. More shots.

It wasn't easy on the city streets, but the wolves survived by attacking unsuspecting hot dog carts or halal trucks. Finding no natural water, the wolves developed a taste for kombucha and locally roasted organic shade grown coffee. By Christmas Day, they were living without predators in the sewers. The quiet was worth the filth.

So they became sewer wolves, moving silently through the lowest shafts beneath the city. Each night around closing time, they would raid a dumpster outside Ray's Famous Pizza. Or burst apart the trash cans of a McDonald's. Still these wolves dreamt of blueberry skies and the ground stupid with leaves and moss. The taste of the air in the forests they had grown up in. They didn't understand opera, but they hoped to.

One day, having no happiness, the wolves howled amongst themselves about how they used to enjoy stealing toddlers that were left unattended on the edge of the forest or crawling through a field of flowers, back when fields with flowers had been a thing. They howled about how they used to raise these children as their own in the forest. It used to be fun.

Sometimes the toddlers would grow into fierce warriors and be two-legged comrades to the wolves, helping them hunt and sometimes coming back to the wolf pack after a scouting mission, to sing the new rock 'n' roll songs of the day. Other times the toddlers grew up to be annoying, and the wolves could eat them for a few meals. It was a win-win.

The wolves didn't have much trouble capturing a baby.

There was a park above the sewer lid and it was as easy as pushing the lid up and just nabbing a kid out of the stroller. Then, look at them all down there in the sewers, nine wolves just smiling down at a screaming baby girl covered in sewage.

They were all friends right away.

The child's parents realized she was gone almost immediately, but had no clue how. The police pretended they were without leads because it wasn't in their job description to have to go down into the sewers. The department of sanitation told the police it wasn't in their job description because they didn't want to battle sewer wolves. So mum was the word.

The parents hung signs all over the city. The parents put up Facebook posts. Tweets. Local TV spots. Craigslist Missed Connection: You Were Our Beloved Baby Girl And You Vanished While We Took A Selfie In Front of the Fountain, Each Day Now Our Tears Could Fill That Fountain …

The wolves kept being wolves and life was pretty much the same for them except now they were listening to National Public Radio and were becoming increasingly liberal in their political beliefs.

Sewer Baby began to walk. Sewer Baby began to talk Wolf. In a way so alien to the human race, she flourished. Sewer Baby played with matches she found, and the wolves sang with happiness when her firelight flickered in their dense, shared darkness.

The girl's parents, having lost all hope of her return, left the city.

A forest had been cleared and a new highway opened. Seeming to sprout overnight, a house popped up for them out of the dewy sod. The family wallpapered themselves in this new house. They plastered themselves in it too. They took out a loan for a Jacuzzi, and after much trouble, had another baby. The family loved the new baby. A girl. And they named the girl the same name as the baby that had been stolen by the wolves.

Each day was a puzzle briefly shining in whatever was the sunlight.

And each night was a maze lit by mostly nothing.

And so they all forgot.

They all forgot who they were and where they'd come from.

It was too painful to remember how beautiful things had been.

31,028

"FUCK EVERYBODY WHO EMAILS ME," I, BUD SMITH said.

3

Goblin

MY NEIGHBORS HAD THE MOST BEAUTIFUL painting hanging in their house. I liked to look at it.

But I was never invited over. People in general were leery of me. You know, some people just don't know how to joke. Some people only know how.

Maybe they thought I was a joke. It's understandable. Anymore, I just stood forever on my front lawn in a rubber monster costume, sweating in the heat.

I'd worn that costume every day since my brother died. The perspiration rolling off me and collecting inside the rubber shell. Staying there. Stuck.

But at certain dusks I was known to fill a juice cup and tread across the street onto my neighbor's perfect lawn.

As the crickets began to sing—I crept to the edge of their house.

As the crickets began to sing—moon hooked hard into the charcoal sky.

I leaned against the window, and watched the woman dancing naked. Surprise. She was doing some glorious ballerina routine all through the house. Twirling. Leaping. How you spell it? Peer-o-what?

The spider plants swayed in their macrame baskets suspended from the ceiling. Once or twice through the glass, I had heard the Steinway piano make a ghost note as she came down to the hardwood floor on a trained big toe.

I had a delusion that her husband was a vacuum cleaner salesman but the vacuums were used for sucking the souls out of a sleeping person. Keeping. But the undeniable truth was that he did own nine different pairs of identical beige dress pants.

And my neighbor's wife, Molly, well Molly cried the loudest at Dale's funeral. But my brother died mysteriously. What's more mysterious? A person's death, or a person's life?

Molly is beautiful in the same way an avalanche crushing over extravagant man-made engineering is beautiful.

Beautiful in the same way as an electrified emerald sea bursting through the gates of a baseball stadium, washing away all the plastic seats, concession stands of hot dogs, popcorns and lite beers.

She did a Grande Jeté from the sectional couch to the glass top coffee table and bounded down the hall like dawn invading the unsuspecting sleepyhead world.

I'd come there for the painting hanging on the wall all alone. See it there it is hanging above the fireplace?

Oil on canvas. Sloppy. 30" by 20". Two boys, crouched, scooping up spiky seed balls from the sweet gum trees.

Of course I recognize those handsome boys.

One boy in a blue straw hat with a black eye and missing a canine tooth, that one be me. Other boy, well, that be, Dale. With braces and wearing the novelty tuxedo t-shirt my father got married in, six sizes too big. Dale is still wearing that shirt, just now he's underground in a pine box.

It's like whoever painted the painting took a polaroid of me and my brother in the summer yard where we grew up, and recreated it here in the neighbor-who-hates-me's house.

And I pulled open the stubborn window. Climbing in. Head then arm then arm then leg and leg. My rubber suit moaned as I dragged it and me across the windowsill into the room. Just like getting born.

Sliding down onto the carpet and crawling across the floor. Glee grin terror. With both arms greedy and quick, I plucked the painting off the wall.

Buried my nose in it. Studied it.

Somehow, there my brother and I were, picking up alien eggs, red seed pods. Young. Dumb. Kids loose in personal paradise.

And while the avalanche wife hurled herself through the rest of the ripe house, I climbed back outside the window, into the life that doesn't have wine or roses or openmouthed kisses for moi.

My plan was to dig up my brother that night and stuff the painting in his coffin. Jump start his heart. I crawled across the lawn like a jail-broke crab.

While I thought about how far it was to the cemetery, I stayed crouched on my driveway. Bouncing in place. The painting face down on hot asphalt.

Thinking. Thinking.

But there to bother me, was a lone cricket in the careening moonlight.

"Helllllllo, baby" I said, placing my cupped hand down on the thing, incredibly slow.

Over insect.

Catch insect.

Make a fist.

The cricket was quiet, was blending in with me. The rotation of earth. The shimmer of stars. The pulse of electric voids.

I put the cricket in my mouth. Crunched down.

Quiet again. Could go back to thinking.

And the soul sucking vacuum cleaner salesman came home in his miracle of a silver spaceship car, so I stood up, and flung the painting onto the shadow soaked-roof of the house I called my home.

He looked over as he passed, fumbling with his keys out of ignorance. His house was unlocked. Even I knew that. He waved.

I said nothing.

I was going to kill him.

Not right then.

I mean sometime when he was really distracted. Maybe when he's opening his birthday present or something. Possibly Christmas morning.

I thought, maybe later, my brother will be awake in his coffin and help me.

With everything.

Wither everything.

But my neighbor stopped at the foot of his garage and showed me unexpected kindness.

"Yo, Greg—what's with the Halloween costume? It's August ... Aren't you hot?"

I show my teeth. Every single one.

"Everything okay?"

I can feel foam gathering in my throat.

He walks out into the street. Stops halfway though. My glasses fog up from the heat escaping out of the rubber suit.

I'm a chainsaw gonna eviscerate you.

"Need anything?"

Gggg-g-g-gggrrrrrrrrowwlllll.

"Know you've been through the ringer. Just wanted to say that if you need anything, anything at all, me and Molly are always here for you. Just across the street, man. Talk or borrow an egg or ten, even pop some cold ones if you like."

He can't tell, I'm doing my silent scream.

"Okay, man, have a nice night ... Just remember, you have a friend in me," he said.

He backed away slowly, and I bet he even had 911 memorized. The little lamb.

The little lamb finally goes inside.

By the time he shuts his door, there is his wife, dressed fully in plum, hair in bun, sitting on the piano bench reading a magazine about famous escapes from jungle prison camps.

I scaled the lattice work, almost ripped my own gutter off getting onto my roof, but when I had the painting in my hands, don't you know I was a flying squirrel, as if each cloud had a vine hanging down for me to swing on.

The cemetery was empty. I borrowed the keys to an excavation machine. Tame yellow metal elephant.

A couple scoops of earth and then I had to borrow a shovel from the tool shed to finish the work. As the sun erased the ink from the world and brought daytime, I reached Dale's coffin, knocked once, twice, thrice. The lid popped up. I shoved the painting into his dead face.

Dale sat up in his coffin and said, "Alien eggs." He gripped the painting to his chest. He kissed the back of the painting.

I hugged him, dusted him off as he coughed, said, "Bro. I know."

"Why you dressed in that rubber suit?"

"Just a phase, they insist. Why you wearing that joke t-shirt?"

He shook his head and pulled a clump of moss from his tuxedo print chest. "Life was a joke. It's cool now though 'cause it's over."

I extended a hand down to Dale and he took it, and climbed up out of his grave, sniffing the air, looking sleepy like someone disturbed from too long of a nap.

He plopped down on the grass next to his open burial plot as if reluctant to leave, his feet still dangling in the hole.

"How'd you die?"

"Me," he said.

"That was some people's theory, I said they were all crazy."

"They were right, and you're probably crazy." He laughed and shoved me. I shoved him back, but stopped his fall with my foot before he slid back in his hole in the ground.

He laughed again, "My hero. Got any bubble gum?"

"Nah," I said. When he was alive Dale always had a piece of watermelon gum in his mouth. "Question for you. Who painted this painting?"

"I did."

"You don't paint."

"Everyone is full of surprises," he said. "I used to juggle too … I could keep a couple lemons up in the air. What secret talents do you have little bro?"

"Nothing."

"Nothing? I doubt that. Ah, find something, man. Find it quick and get on with things."

"I can't believe you could paint that good …"

He looked down at the painting. "I painted the front, that's you and me in grandma's yard … and my girlfriend painted the back …"

I didn't realize there was anything on the back.

He flipped the painting over and there was Molly painted on the reverse side of the canvas. She was nude, as usual, but dancing, suspended in an orange tornado that was passing over endless jail yards, gray and brown, with barbed wire fences and people in striped white and black jumpsuits trying to play basketball with flat basketballs.

I was ready to call this family reunion. Headlocks and shit talk. My brother is back! Like—here's your only warning: Me and bro gonna burn down this town. Your dusty house first.

But Dale said, "Alright pal, I'm gonna go back in the ground now. Have a nice rest of your life." He kissed me on the side of my head, and damn he stunk. "Lose this costume," he said, "it's not your style."

"I like it, helps me remember you …"

"Don't." My brother reached over and grabbed the mask just beneath my right eye slit. My glasses went flying into the grass and everything blurred. As he yanked, the costume ripped and pulled from my head like a dark flower blossom opening.

I felt the breeze on my neck and my chest and then my belly as the rubber split. With both hands now, Dale ripped the suit off me, and in doing so, he fell back into his own coffin and laughed again.

I put my glasses back on. Dale was flat on his back, smirking.

"Why'd you kill yourself?"

He opened one eye and grinned.

"It's private."

He stood up and gave me a look just like he used to do when he was a little kid and he was happy because he knew something I didn't know. "If I wanted anybody to know I would have written a note."

"If you had written that in a note I wouldn't have had to come and dig you up …"

"Didn't ask you to dig me up. Well hold on, maybe I do have a scrap of paper with some more info for you, uh, maybe it's here in one of my pockets, let me look, I don't recall." He stuck his hands in his pocket and looked surprised, "Oh! Here it is!"

He stuck his hand up and there wasn't a note, he was just giving me the bird. The skin was gone from the hand, maybe it was in his pocket now.

"Love you, dude. Don't take this raw, but I hope I don't see you for a hundred more years. And please, tell Molly I'm waiting for her in that place we dreamed about."

He sat down and closed his own coffin from the inside. The painting was in there with him. Just as well.

I waited for a while to see if he would come back out, but he didn't. I even called his name and sung his favorite song. But then, a couple feral dogs had appeared at the edge of the cemetery and I worried that they'd eat him if I left my post as quasi-guard, so I covered the grave back up with dirt.

On my walk home, the sun came out and almost set my pale body on fire. Skin so milky that hadn't seen the sun's light for so long.

I walked bare assed into town. Nude and getting my senses back. Admiring things. The stained glass in the church windows. The mailbox covered in little silly seashells. The sound of someone playing a saxophone in their garage. But only once did I stop. I stood in the sprinklers that were raging outside the funeral home. The spray whipping against me when I got closer. The water so cool. I let it soak me. A cat watched me on the edge of the lawn. After a while it licked the back of its paw and began to repair itself, too.

Schwimps

THE ALBINO GOT DRUNK AND CAPTURED A flamingo. I mean, there was a lot leading up to it, I'll tell you some. There was a whole life, really. He put in for time off from work. He had a factory job putting wood modeling glue in plastic containers. They liked him there. He was the star. He shook everyone's hands, and got on a bus from Duluth, Minnesota, where he was born. He took the bus all the way down to the Everglades, a burlap sack sitting on his lap.

The albino liked to dress like Buddy Holly, a little bit of a fetish. He once told human resources that he considered himself the reincarnation of the singer, but eh, he wasn't going to do anything about it.

The bus ride took three days but he'd never seen the country, and so was starstruck by the average scenery and all the truck stops along the route. And the country was bland, and was fine, and was ugly, and was just staggering. They stopped in Des Moines, and ate at a cafe across the street from The World's Second Biggest Ball of String. The man stood staring at the ball of string for a while, kind of irrationally mad at it. The bus driver yelled at him and broke his trance. After that they stopped in Quincy—Quincy, haha, big shit. Quincy.

They spent the night in Nashville and he went to the Grande Ole Opry. After the tour of the Opry, he broke away from the group and had relations with a Mexican prostitute who was costumed up like Dolly Parton. He said what's your real name, she said, "Dolly Parton." She had fucked him for half price, she claimed, just for the fun and experience of being with an albino. She took polaroid photos with him during and after, laughing and saying, "These will be great for my portfolio." He felt exploited. He felt embarrassed to feel exploited, knowing she was exploited too. Everyone under the sun was exploited. I am and you are, too. He said, "See you later, Dolly." She said, "See ya later, Buddy."

He decided he wanted a change. He would dye his hair red like his dead hero. He walked down the street towards the glowing lights of the pharmacy. Everything was a miracle—internal and external.

A car headed towards the train tracks slammed on the brakes at the last second. Burnt rubber. The train thundering across the road. The wooden crossing arm must have malfunctioned and not lowered down. God! An elderly woman had seen this near catastrophe and she yelled at the driver in the green Prius, "You're a lucky sonofabitch!" The driver yelled back, laughing, pointing at the train still blazing past. "Ah, don't I know it!" The albino said, "I know it too!" And the elderly woman looked at him like he didn't belong and the driver hung out of the window too and looked at the albino like he didn't belong.

He walked into the pharmacy, a lonely brick building, feeling fine anyway. They had airplane pillows. He bought one for the bus, and walked out of the store with it around his neck. But then on the way back from the drug store he was robbed by two junkies, a man and a woman who came out from the dumpster like wraiths. He had to hand over the plastic bag with the hair dye and the potato chips and new insoles for his sneakers. The thieves let him keep the airplane pillow, maybe thinking it was a neck brace or something. The woman sat down on the sidewalk and puked. The man said, "Sam! Get up!" She got up, wiped her mouth, and apologized. The thief was so kind to her, and she was so kind to him. The albino thought, aw they must be in love. The man with the knife was also nice enough, or high enough, to let him keep his wallet, he just had to hand over all the cash in it. $173. So the bus ticket remained. And his Visa Cash Rewards card remained. And his union card remained.

He said goodbye to the thieves, and even shook the man's hand. The woman just grinned, keeping her distance. She said, "Now I've seen it all."

The albino slept in a motel room with a view of another motel across the highway. People over there were having the times of their lives, he could just tell. The time of their lives, he thought. The time of their lives, he thought. He went to sleep and had his reoccurring nightmare that he was being surrounded by flamingos. They pressed in from all sides. They pressed in and knocked him over and climbed all over him. He woke up feeling drained. The air conditioner was murmuring Satanic verses. He looked out the motel window at the view of the other motel. All the lights were off over there now. The time of their lives, he thought. The time of their lives, he thought.

In the morning, back on the bus after a plate of eggs and grits, he philosophized, Oh the things you can do with corn, you can do anything with corn. He started talking to the person in the seat in front of him. A man from Devil's Lake, North Dakota who was on his way to see his grandchildren in Pensacola. At first the man from Devil's Lake was such an enthusiastic talker, and travel companion but the problem was he kept having to turn around to make conversation with the albino and between the combination of the man from Devil's Lake developing a crick in his neck, and the raised ire of his seat mate, a teenaged goth who was sketching in her pad with aggressive spasms, the talk waned and the albino could tell he should shut up. So he shut up.

In the lingering silence that followed, the albino decided maybe he'd transform into a person who designed billboards. Look at all of them stuck on the side of the interstate like wild flowers. So easy. Put anything you want at all on them and all the people driving by could do nothing but say thank you thank you, praise you by gobbling up your products, whatever they may be. They'd fall right under your spell.

When he got off the Greyhound bus in humid humid humid dripping sweat Florida, all he saw was concrete and the concrete dismayed him. He waited outside the accordion door and said goodbye to all the other passengers as they exited the bus, even re-entering to shake hands with the driver, who said, "Now you take care of yourself, Mr. Holly."

The depot was like a war zone. But a black boy was leaning against a rusted van in the depot parking lot. The boy said, "Taxi." And the albino said, "Hey give me a ride to the swamp for money." The boy said a sum that seemed way too high and the albino said, "Black boy, you'll drive me for half that or no deal." The boy walked up with a congenial look on his face, and then he just slapped Buddy—I guess that's what we are calling him now. O! He slapped Buddy hard on the face and then the boy danced back, going O! O! But there was no audience. And the wind had started whipping. He missed Dolly Parton.

When the man came at the boy, he got slapped again and that was the end of that. "Don't call me that, you fuggin' vampire." The albino said he was sorry. He got money out of the ATM, gave it to the child. Then they journeyed on together.

"What do you want to be called?" The boy didn't answer, right away. But after he turned the key and the engine started knocking, he said, "I wanna be treated like anybody wants to be treated—with respect." Buddy nodded.

And then the child drove, barely being able to see above the steering wheel of the van. And as he drove on he continued with his line of speech, "I saw on TV, this show about people who hunt pale human ghosts like you in the jungle. They kill your ass. You're a trophy to them."

The albino said, "I saw that show, too. People collect anything I guess. I'm magic. Whoo-hoo. My hands and feet are worth quite a lot. They pay top dollar for my privates parts."

The child said, "Now don't let it go to your ego. It's just old world superstition. Here in America, you're worthless, baby."

Buddy had a map and cheeks that stung, and newfound respect; and the man maybe was magic. He was learning. He was taught. There was beer in the van that the albino promised to replace. The child was worried his stepdad would not be happy, but then remembered that man was never happy.

They drove on, the passenger side headlight flickering on and off, on and off. An electrical problem. Buddy said politely, "Please turn up here." The boy said, "Why sure." And turned and hummed. The boy's name was Maurice, he finally said. As he drove farther into the Everglades, Buddy drank beer after beer, throwing the silver cans onto the marsh beside the narrow road.

Maurice wondered if the man would try to kill him. Try, haha. It was a nice place to get murdered, he thought. So peaceful. So serene. First they saw the white ibis through the sawtooth grass. Maurice said, "You if you was a bird, spitting image." The albino remained quiet.

And then he saw the pink flash of the mimosa blossom, all alien and feathery. And then there they were, three flamingos together walking through the mud. "Stop the van." Maurice pressed the brake.

Buddy got out and stood at the edge of the muddy water, the burlap sack in one shaking hand, the beer can in the other perfectly still hand. He coughed and the flamingos looked over at him and stared back at the flamingos, until they finally looked away. He'd been dreaming about them. Every night he had a normal dream, where something good would be happening, maybe he'd be joking with his first wife and she'd be laughing, or he'd be climbing a mountain to collect whatever the prize in the dream was, and then suddenly the dream would be interrupted by flamingos who just kept pushing into the frame, jerking around and honking. The three flamingos were so pink and they looked just like they belonged in National Geographic, only, and not the real world.

But then in the corner of his eye he saw there was a fourth flamingo. But this one was malnourished and there was something wrong with its coat. It was a sickly pale. The albino threw his beer can into the mud, and launched into the water and the healthy flamingos scattered. Maurice shouted, "Stop!" The pink flamingos got away but the white flamingo got one of its feet lodged on some trash that was floating in the water and the bird was anchored. He put the burlap sack over its head and the bird screamed once and then was deathly quiet. The man carried the thrashing flamingo to the van.

The boy said, "Now fuck you, I ain't driving!" Buddy said, "I'll drive, then." Maurice tried to slap Buddy but he pulled back and Maurice hit the bird in the chest and it hissed, and he was sorry. "I just want to feed the thing some shrimp, goddammit, Maurice."

Maurice said. "You're not gonna hurt it, I'll see to that!" The bird was put gently into the back of the van. "I'm not gonna hurt anything." The doors were closed. The man said, "It's getting late, let's go." He climbed behind the wheel and the two of them drove twenty minutes towards civilization. Maurice was giving directions now. It's always faster to go back the way you came, than it is to come out into the unknown.

He directed the man to a neon light food stand on the side of the road that sold boiled craw, shrimp cocktail, scallops, any fried fish you want. The albino bought two pounds of raw shrimp with the heads still on them and fed it to the flamingo in the back of the van. The bird was happy the bag was off its head. Munched up the shrimp. The bird shit in the van. The bird looked around the van like the van was its new home. The bird looked okay with it. No predators and they feed me shrimp. The bird vomited. The bird shit again.

Maurice said he didn't care it was his fake father's van. The sun fell. The half moon came up. It was just a sliver in the sky. Buddy wondered where the World's Biggest Ball of String was. And wasn't it always changing? The flamingo slept. Just as the food stand closed for the night, Buddy bought the boy a fried catfish sandwich and a sarsaparilla, said, "Your tip." Maurice said, "Oh lucky me." The albino's feet hurt and he wished he had his insoles, "What now?" Buddy said.

A cop car drove through the lot but kept going, taking the easy short cut to the other county road. Maurice said, "What now? I don't know. It would have been easier to bring the shrimp to the bird and not the bird to the shrimp, not the other way around. You're stupid."

The albino said, "You're bright."

Maurice said, "Let's take it back." It being this sickly creature. Let's take it back to the wild. Let's let it continue its sickness in the maw of nature. The pale man agreed. He popped the last beer, and then handed over a twenty dollar bill to the boy even though the beer couldn't have been more than half that. He was on vacation. Money just falls out of everywhere when you're on vacation. Buddy said, "Let's go, let's bring this poor thing home. And we'll get to enjoy how the stars shine out there in the boonies," he said. "I'm curious to know."

The child laughed. "If you don't know how the stars shine by now, no experience is ever going to help."

"What?"

"Either you know, or you don't know."

'Then I don't know, motherfucker."

"You don't. Congratulations. And you never will." Buddy shook the child's tiny hand. Then he went around the side of the restaurant to use the toilet. And he wondered if Devil's Lake was as cursed as it sounded. And he wondered if anyone had been killed by that train yet. If not yet, then like all things, soon. As he opened the squeaky restroom door he heard the van start, and he kind of grunted in accepted defeat. When he came back, refreshed, the van was long gone. The diseased, white flamingo was standing in the middle of the parking lot. A fluorescent light was shining down on it, making the flamingo glow like some kind of long-necked seraph, doomed to roam the earth. A misplaced angel, cast off from everything.

And the angel looked straight at Buddy, and went honk, honk, honk, honk.

Buddy stared back and the flamingo didn't look away.

You ever wonder why you are beautiful?

You ever ask anybody?

Nah?

Well, me neither.

Good Gravy

ONE TIME DANIELLE SHOT ME IN THE CHEST WITH A derringer pistol. So we broke up. I wasn't mad. She must have thought I was somebody else. I let her down in some magic way. Danielle was a world class piano player, and she has a body someone would have made a statue of a long time ago. Now, statues aren't as popular. Her bullet hit me in my passenger side tit, wedged to a hard stop at my scapula, oh god. I called a taxi cab and pretended I was on the way home from a costume party. My costume was: 'person bleeding to death from some lovely mistake.' The most embarrassing part of the whole ordeal was when I got lucid again, in the shiny bowels of the hospital, I realized I was wearing flip flops. I hid both my feet from the staff. My health insurance was expired, so the doctor just sewed me up, leaving the hunk of ammunition inside me, apologizing the whole time for being rich, and apologizing for me being poor. I said, "How many hours a week do you work?" The doctor thought. "Hmmm. Three hundred hours." I almost fell off the operating table. I said, "That's not being rich!" He pulled out his prescription pad and kissed it. Then he tore the sheet off and gave it to me. I still have it. One of my finest trophies I ever got from a misunderstanding. After that he called the nurse in and pointed at my bloody feet. She came back with a pail of warm water and washed the blood off. Painted my toenails as green as Ireland looks on TV in that famous soap commercial. I went home. My other girlfriend was studying to be a surgeon. She was starting with horses for practice. She had all these books, and surgical supplies she'd gotten from a rancher who was put out of business by whatever puts a rancher out of business. Vegetables? Subway systems? Blue skies no longer being such a sexy fad? Kim is such a goddamn empath, she was weeping for me as she dug the bullet out. But I might as well have been dead. I didn't care. And then she showed me the bullet. It was scrunched up funny, twisted like a cigarette butt with all the love sucked from it. The bullet had a name written on it but we didn't even know the person, yet there they were, written on the offending slug of doom. So as the story goes, Kim took the bullet over to Danielle's house. She was shaking with this fear of the worst not being over. I laughed at that, because comfort is just a thing you drink. Or a thing you pull off a shelf out of the dark and it tries to light you up but often fails and you stay dark forever. Or a thing that is leaving you, and you just involuntarily wave goodbye and you don't even know you're doing it. Train cresting a hill, and you're shrinking back. And this vengeful horse surgeon, I joked, this vengeful horse surgeon, well she was the one who was so very brave and yelling on the porch in the thunder and the lightning, screaming at Danielle, "I'm bursting with love, don't do that again! If you're gonna shoot anyone, shoot me dead right here!" This kind of spectacle made Danielle take a step back into the mysterious house, but she came forward again, angry, screaming, "I wasn't gonna shoot anybody else, but now you've inspired me!" There was some fumbling for the pistol and in this fumble, Kim burst through the screen door, splitting it, shredding it. She chopped off Danielle's trigger finger with an equestrian scalpel. A small sword, really. Danielle lay there whimpering for her future. "There how you like that? You artless thing." Kim took the finger and left. Back in the living room, I sat down and drank raspberry tea with gin, and the rain came down for me too. The stereo was playing a Ted Hawkins cassette. *How many of you people tonight can testify that your baby tastes like good gravy?* I'd taken this opportunity to call Henry, who came over and changed my bandages. He's so handsome. About as pretty as four of those doctors smashed into one person. And he hasn't worked 300 hours in his whole life. He's the laziest guy who isn't in a cemetery. Henry peeled the bandages off me, greedily. He saved those bandages, because he's weird like that. He's got a collection of the fingerprints of whoever he's ever been sweet on. He'll take those fingerprints while somebody is just snoozing away. Wake up with inky hands and you don't know why, but then you remember someone is sweet on you, and it's alright, it's worth it. So what if this life is hurtful? So what the bullet didn't even have your name on it? So what the horses were laid off, and now walk along the dusty stretch of highway looking for a job? So what if all the taxi cab drivers are cursing and scrubbing dried blood from the backseats of the world they were tricked into carrying a fare through? All my friends and enemies are winded from chasing they don't even know what, and maybe I'm leading the league in disappointment, disaffection, vibrant misery, and smiling ugliness. I can't begin to weigh how many pounds of air I've had stolen from my lungs by people who love but don't care to know why. Or hate and have the problem of understanding why. When Kim walked in the door, she was shaking Danielle's finger in the air, all proud. No more concertos for that creature. But hey, lose yourself, transform into something else, that's how I try to live. Henry took the finger from her and put it in his bleach-stinking work shirt pocket, said, "Thank you." I was feeling weak. I said thank you, too. The next week I got an itemized bill from the hospital. Turns out they charge you over a grand to get an emergency pedicure. I've heard the sun makes the wild flowers and spiky weeds grow like a fat carpet on everything they can talk into it. I've heard the sun dries up the earth and turns it to a desert, or an exposed and bashful river bed. Fuck me. Fuck you. You've gotta try to love things, even if they just want to eat your heart while you sit there watching them do it, coerced, dying laughing.

Everybody's Darlin'

I BECAME A MINOR CELEBRITY AROUND TOWN after the police threw me through the plate glass window of the porno shop.

Traffic was stopped. Everyone saw.

There was bursting glass. And there was me soaring headfirst onto the sidewalk.

When I staggered to my feet, those pigs were still standing in the store, looking down at me. I was finally out in the sunshine though, while they remained in the shadows. I'd committed no crime, so I yelled, "Well what now?"

"Get going," one of the cops said. He kicked more glass at me.

The other cop shook his head, zipped his fly.

It was a complete surprise when I wasn't arrested. I guess all my leaky crimson and the embarrassment was enough.

It usually goes like this:

Live Your Life + Intersect With Other Lives = Wake Up In Jail.

But this one time, I was walking on. Kicking my sneakers in front of me through the gravel headed towards whatever else the sun and moon and stars had going on.

A mustard-colored convertible pulled out of the gridlock. And a girl was yelling, "Dude! I just saw the whole thing!"

"Did you now?"

She unlatched the door.

"Get in."

"I'm a fountain of blood, you don't want that in your car."

She motioned again. I climbed in and glass fell out of my hair and my shirt and my face.

"This isn't my car, this is my stepmother's car. Bleed all you want in my stepmother's car."

We drove behind the porno shop. A narrow path. Branches slapping the windshield made me flinch, but she didn't flinch. Some people are born numb.

But in the trees, all sap covered and weather-faded, I saw a blow up doll someone had resurrected from the dumpster, and hung there in the dead branches, lying horizontal flying like Superman or Superwoman. I pointed up, but the girl didn't lose a beat.

"I see that every day," she said, and just kept cruising. "Hey why'd they do that? Why'd they throw you through the window?"

"I walked in the backroom and caught those cops masturbating on a guy they'd handcuffed. Having some kind of a race."

"That's what our tax dollars are for?"

"Some of them, anyway." I wiped my bloody brow, quivering. Adrenaline gone and me suddenly overtaken by weakness. "I was just looking for a quiet place to get high."

The girl nodded. "10-4."

We hit a whoopdee, the car flew.

"This is fun," she said. "I feel alive."

"Oh, what's that like?"

The car crashed down. Each of my inner organs became a pinball of meat bouncing against other pinballs of meat. I was at my limit and bent over, so my forehead pressed against the dash.

"Shit, please pull over," I gasped.

"Sure."

She slammed the brakes. Dust engulfed us, catching back up to us.

"I'm in massive pain, it'd help if I could inject some of the medicine I have in my pocket."

She spun side saddle on the bench seat and faced me like I was the main feature in a movie house. People can romanticize anything. "I've never seen a real life junky before," she said.

"We're a dying breed."

She was all smiles. Beanpole skinny. Giant glasses. Thin hair. So unsexy, and at the same time just the sexiest thing.

"Need my belt?"

She took her belt off, handed it to me. Butterflies all over the belt. I ran my fingers across one's wings. But I didn't need her belt and gave it back.

I took my gear from my fanny pack. Needle and tourniquet. Then I began the real work with lighter and cotton ball. She had out a notepad and she jotted notes with a pen that had the logo of her university on it.

"This is very exciting! I might do my thesis on this."

"Neato."

"I'm a Drug Studies Major," she said.

"Professor'll love it. A Plus Plus Plus."

I slid the needle in, pushed the plunger.

Then we were in the golden hour. We were track and field stars. She was the Statue of Liberty sandblasted and shined up and shrunk down to the size of an ordinary Miss America. My blood that was still pouring out of me wasn't blood anymore, it was honey and Miss America was a beekeeper and I was making her money. She'd collect it and sell it to somebody.

"Tell me more about yourself ..."

I sighed. I said, "Here's some free honey for you. In a dream I had one time, I used to own that porno shop."

"Oh, what's it like selling sexual happiness in a dream state?"

"Two truths about dildos I'll say to you. Miserable people don't own a single dildo ..." I blinked. I blinked again. Everything was glorious one second and then the next second I was asleep.

I woke up on a miniature couch, a folk band hellishly playing in the corner. A tall woman playing an electric harp. A short man fingering a washtub bass. Someone unseen, yodeling.

When I die, if it is today, if it is tomorrow, will someone please write At Least He Hated Folk Music on my tombstone.

Also let it be noted, I didn't like folks.

The room was packed with folks, and the room kept closing in, but it wasn't my fault. It was a college dormitory, not much larger than a jail cell. I panicked like I was covered in fire ants. I leapt up on the couch from a prone position to a standing one so my skull cracked the ceiling and almost knocked me back out.

Below me there were what seemed like hundreds of slimy-faced students in grandma underwear, pimples and creative facial hair, and shaking plastic cups so wine and beer sloshed everywhere and all over their own sweaty bodies. They were beyond thrilled that I was awake and I'm not used to that.

The band stopped. The students cheered.

The girl from earlier was topless and holding a microphone.

"Everyone, this is my friend! Meet my extraordinary friend!" The microphone squealed through a tiny amplifier as she told the party I was the most interesting person they'd ever meet.

"... Like a character from a JT Slazenger short story."

I said, "Who the hell is JT Slazenger?"

"... Launched through a brick wall by a riot squad."

"Not true."

"... Filled his entire body with cyanide in my stepbrother's car."

"Also not true."

"... After that he shit himself but it's alright."

I reached down my pants and my underwear was gone, so maybe that one had happened.

I jumped down from the couch. Students latched on, I couldn't pry them off. My elbows and knees did nothing.

The girl shouted, "Don't get mad! You're the guest of honor!"

Vomit bubbled up my throat.

They all moved then.

I vomited my way out of the room, vomited my way into the hallway, ruining all those academic rugs all along the way.

Now I was wandering the maze of the quad, no idea how to exit. I stumbled past a room of kids, with their door open, drinking beer, watching a kung fu film.

"How do I get out?"

"Yo," one dude said, standing up and shutting the door in my face. "You just get out!" he yelled through the closed door.

That's one way.

Next stop on my journey, I discovered a silver water fountain and washed my mouth out.

A boy saw me. He was sitting crisscross applesauce, possibly meditating under a window with utter blackness leaking through the window and into the fluorescent building of higher learning.

"You good?" the boy said.

"I'm fine," I said, touching my broken face. I sat down on the floor some distance across from him.

"You don't go to school here?" he said.

"I don't go to school here, no," I said. "I'm a visitor from the outside world. Cops beat the shit out of me."

He said, "I'm a visitor too. My girlfriend is at some weird ass party. I came out here for some peace and quiet."

I said, "I guess I did too."

"Why did the cops beat you up?"

"Caught them being cops," I said, and laughed. "They like to be cops in secret."

"They beat you without due process?"

"Um, maybe, I don't know. What's the process like for beating somebody up?"

"If you want to legally beat someone's ass you have to do it in Las Vegas live on pay per view. You have to be in the ring, with gloves on—there has to be millions of dollars on the line. You have to have a corner man. You have to have a mouth guard in. Was it like that?"

I said, "No. This wasn't in Las Vegas. This wasn't live on pay per view."

"Then what they did was illegal," he said. "I should know. I studied law. I'm going to be a lawyer. Tomorrow I take the bar exam."

"Righteous," I said, and my guts started to pulse again. "You'll be great. I can just tell."

He said, "Give me your hand, brother."

I had enough strength and sense to hold my hand out. He wrote a phone number on the back of my hand.

"For next time," he said. "You just call me when you're in trouble and I'll come on down there and I'll be your representative, your spirit guide, your sherpa up the impossible mountain climb of your own life."

I was dumbfounded.

"You want to help people," I said, kind of in dizzy disbelief. "That's incredible. I've met almost every single kind of animal in the zoo, I've met the animal that wants to hide; the animal that wants to steal; the animal that wants to hurt; this is my first time encountering the animal that wants to be my lawyer."

The kid smiled. He said, "I'm the animal that wants to be your friend."

Jangle Bell

I FELL INTO SOME BAD LUCK, SO I WENT TO SEE THE black magic priestess on Jackson Street. She charged $5, had a storefront across from the hat shop.

Her store was packed with faux fog, and an artificial birch tree forest. Just follow the glowing lantern to the back. Ignore the recording of crows cawwwing.

Like all aspects of being alive, this too, was a little too much.

Funny though, I remembered when the place was the Sunny Cup tire shop. Just one set of defective tires was all it took. After that this was a travel agency. Wanna go to monsoon rainforests, or the edge of an endless desert? Speak to the man in the suit and the tie.

Now it seems, any dummy can be in charge of their own ceaselessly pleasurable destiny.

I made it through. I entered the priestess' tent. Fragrent smoke wrapped around me. She wore a low cut blouse, covered in cosmetic gore jewelry. There was a special light that made her teeth shine like the moon. Maybe mine did too.

I was given a baby dragon skull to hold, and I did that, pretending I didn't know it was a German Shepherd skull. You know me, I get high with the veterinarian, sometimes. I know things about the animal kingdom.

She asked me what my matter was, and I tucked $7 into her bra and told her, I'd written some stories but I don't know if they are any good. Could she consult the runes or the bones or whatever. Could she tell me their quality?

Well what are the stories? she said in a tired wheeze.

Well, I said, I wrote one story about a man who finds a severed head in the parking lot of where he works. It's a really good looking head, long-locked and high cheekbones, so attractive in fact that he takes the head home and tries to have a three way with the severed head and his wife. The wife is really upset. She always hoped her body was enough sexually for her husband, but she always suspected her body wasn't enough. The story ends with the husband having sex alone with the severed head, and the wife answering an ad on a dating site. The twist is the ad has been sent by the undead body of the severed head, which is still sentient, and just like the woman, still looking for love.

The priestess' eyes rolled to the back of her head so only the whites showed.

I continued with my stories. I said, I wrote another story, similar, about a different woman who finds the same severed head in the cantaloupe pile at the grocery store. The supermarket on Mill Road actually. She too takes the severed head home and suggests a three way with the severed head and her own wife, but the woman's wife, midway through the act, realizes that the severed head is not a woman, rather, a man. She'd always suspected her wife was attracted to men. After the intercourse, things change in the relationship, some things for the better, some things for the worse. That's life. That story has no twist, because ya know, that's life. People just grow apart. But instead of letting the head end their relationship, the women bring it back to the supermarket, where it stays for two weeks, slowly rotting until it's thrown out with all the other wasted cantaloupes. In an early draft I made the bold claim that a severed head has no gender, has fluid sexuality, etc. But my writing group kicked me out over that. And they also said it was insensitive of me to insinuate that a polyamorous relationship is not a sustainable one. I said, what the fuck, it's a severed head.

I wrote another story told from the point of view of a severed head that won a MacArthur Genius Grant, but you never get to learn why the head won the MacArthur Grant because that's such a stupid award, and I'm not jealous at all about it. The story is told in the second person. You're the narrator. You're the severed head, at the end of the story. But in the beginning you're a regular so-called genius with a full and useful body that's so good, you're often approached on street corners and propositioned lewdly. You're home one day and open the refrigerator and realize the hot dogs you loved more than anything else in this godforsaken world, are gone. So you go to the store and buy other hot dogs but when you eat them they aren't as good. You realize everything gets worse everyday you are alive. You're such a sensitive baby that you cut your head off with a circular saw and then that story ends with a bunch of different couples taking turns having an orgasm with your beautifully dead perfectly androgynous head.

The black magic priestess shook her head, and her beaded hair sounded like glass rain. She said in a booming voice that shook the tent, these are not good stories! No one would read these stories. Why would you write them?

She was waiting for an answer but I didn't have one.

She said, you need to write stories with a beginning a middle and an end. A three act arc, where the character learns a valuable lesson and undergoes some change. Why not try your hand at a Cinderella story, where the human spirit overcomes? Instead you're just writing about getting jollies off with corpses, that will get you nowhere and the reader will be mad at you.

I listened to her because just over her shoulder was a framed rejection from The New Yorker Magazine. The slip was handwritten, and full of praise for her writing.

In another life, but this life too, she was a different person. And then, I started to wonder what had happened to everyone I ever knew.

It seems that sometimes, people are just walking talking lightning bolts that strike the ground around us and make our hair stand up for a little while. But then they are gone, off to nowhere, off to that place just beyond our range of knowledge. I wanted to touch the priestess' cheek and tell her that she would not survive here in this strip mall, but she must have known that anyway. Those who divine the future for just five bucks, are most doomed of all to eat suffering for breakfast, lunch, and dinner, maybe even a cursed ice cream sundae before bed.

The buzzer buzzed and that meant my private conference was up and she held her hands out and made me give back the baby dragon skull that I was pretending wasn't a German shepherd skull.

I gave her the skull and there was an awkward moment where she inferred I could purchase oral sex in the tent for $35. I told her that before I was over the hill, people used to pay me $50 to put my penis in their mouth. She shook my hand. Said, Congratulations.

I left the tent. As I made my way through the artificial fog and the artificial forest, I saw cars driving slow down Jackson Street. Our town gets smaller every year and I knew all the cars.

I crouched in the fog and sat there like a frog letting the fog wrap around me. I didn't want to exist the way I was. Believe me pal, I'd rather be a freelance animal. Wild. There is no animal more freelance than a slick frog. I'd rather have no memory, no art, no doubt.

Instead, I have to do all these stupid human things with all these stupid human beings. Nothing wants to swoop out of the sky and crack my face apart to slurp my brains out, but I think I'd rather have that happen to me. Put it to you this way, if I could find a hawk big enough to eat me, I'd commit suicide by hawk.

And there it was. I'd just seen my ex pull into the lot of the hat shop and I didn't want to be seen leaving the black magic priestess' store, because my ex would either think I was fucking the priestess or I was cuckoo for going there for advice. I laughed. My ex was still driving around on those Sunny Cup tires. They'd explode sometime.

The fog swirled around me. I could hear the priestess practicing some new incantation. Then her cellphone rang, the ringtone was What A Beautiful World. She let it go, when the shop got quiet again she carried on again.

I waited until my ex walked out of the hat shop, appearing with a new hat sitting right there on that big fat noggin. I watched the car roll away, become invisible again, sucked back into the ugly past where I willingly hid it too.

And then I opened the door so the jangle bell made its cling clang music and I walked down bright and sunny Jackson Street to the bar where I had my notebook of stories hidden between the waterlogged weight lifting encyclopedias on the Formica bookcase. I didn't want anyone at the lumberyard to know I was a writer and no one else working at the lumberyard would ever dream dream dream of going into that bar.

As I cut through the cemetery, leaping over a tombstone, I thought about something else the black magic priestess had said. She'd asked me what the moral of my stories were.

I'd said, actually each story has the same moral: You never have sex with a person, you have sex with the idea of a person.

It was then that her eyes rolled back to normal, the pupils there again, focused on foolish ol' me. One eye was blue, the other gray.

Ahhhh, she'd said, Here's how you fix everything—get rid of all your morals.

E - A - D - G - B - E

I EVEN SLEPT WITH MY PRIZED GUITAR IN MY HANDS.

That's how much I loved it.

But while I was in the shower, Dan Mayweather snuck into my room and took my guitar, so I pursued him across town, thinking he'd be on his porch playing it. But he was not.

Roommate said, "Gone to Chicago."

I wrote down the address and got on a bus but when I knocked on that Chicago door, a tall woman in a purple hat handed me a note.

Note said: 'Tell all wimpy happy-on-the-farm pursuant parties I'm bye bye … shadow-style slipped into blooming dusk, everywhere and nowhere, me and this sweet six string.'

"To where?" I asked the tall woman.

She studied the note. "Hmmm. Is Bye Bye a town in Tennessee?"

I burst into the house. Searched all the rooms till I knew it was true: he wasn't there. In the bathroom, tucked between two magazines, I found a letter from the government addressed to Dan that read: Welcome to the Army!

"He's taken my guitar to the jungle!"

I journeyed backwards to Louisville. Where my girl, Evie, the sweetest singer you ever heard, said, “Forget the guitar. Get another guitar.”

Shook my head, “Need that one. My grandfather carved that guitar himself from a tree that his grandfather had planted. The tree got struck by lightning every time it rained but did not fall, Evie. Stood there proud and tall, till he chopped it down.”

“How we gonna make music?”

I opened my mouth to speak, but just shook my head.

She said to me as the screen door slapped shut, “Nothing belongs to nobody, and I’m slipping through your hands.”

That night I shaved my head and in the morning when the sun was popping over the corn, I went and joined the army too. Not to kill. Or to prove a point for God and country.

Just to find my guitar.

Day One at training:

“Anybody seen a big-eyed Kentucky boy pass through here with a maple body acoustic?”

Day Two at training:

“He’s an ugly guy, big goofy strawberry for a nose, hateful eyes.”

Day Nine:

“He never liked my music. He was always trying to get me to stop, to do other stupid stuff.”

Day Thirty at training:

“He couldn’t pick guitar for anything, you’d know who I’m looking for, bad picker, torture listening to him.”

Day Sixty, on the boat over in crashing tempest of a storm:

“He’s got a dent on his forehead from where we smashed into a tractor, trying to jump it, this was when he was riding on my handlebars, when we was kids, when we was daredevils.”

No luck. No one knew his whereabouts.

So I sunk deeper into death. And in just a week of horror bush kill life, I was all like: “LOOK AT ME—BIG BADASS SOLDIER!” I screamed into the tiger wet drip drop rain-all-the-time jungle.

And while on patrol, machine gun slung low, I thought about the C chord. How easy it was to place the fingers, how anyone could do it. Cavemen could.

I thought about D minor, the pinky, ring, middle and pointer, the sweet dissonance of it, as I was tossing grenades over roofs. D minor no big deal.

I burned a thatched hut village and visualized a F# barre chord.

In all foxholes and caves I yelled for Dan Mayweather.

At leave, in all the depots I asked for Dan Mayweather, at whore houses and in bars with rotted floors.

Stars and stripes superiors and staff sergeant worldwide had not heard of him.

I drew Dan Mayweather's face at Da Nang, beach called My Khe, with a bloody palm. Waves pummeling the surface of my eroded earth.

I dreamt of the B major, hovering in a ping-pong waterfall.

And one night, awoken by someone strumming, exotically, I climbed up from my bed in the palm fronds and crawled through big thick mud, to peer out at our own enemy sitting in the middle of a downpour, playing a song.

I raised my rifle.

But could not fire.

The song was too sweet. Though I do not know its name.

I crawled back and went to bed.

The next morning there were explosions all around. And planes that dropped fire bombs on us wrongly. Our own damn planes.

I leapt into a river and the rapids took me away farther still from my life on the farm.

I too became a shadow on the edge of the villages. I hid. I did not travel in daylight. I stowed away on a ship leaving the war. Felt no remorse.

I was in a Dutch hostel, having lost all trace of Dan Mayweather. He used to rattle on about Amsterdam and red lights, but I couldn't find him here, and I had knocked on every red window. I looked out of my window, down onto the lamp-lit streets, and felt defeated. I had nowhere to go next.

A note slipped under the door.

"I've taken your guitar to the top of Mt. Everest, it's always been a dream of mine."

I ran out into the hallway, I ran down into the street. There were no people.

The Sherpa mountaineers tried to talk me out of the climb. They said I did not have the proper training. They said the air would be thin and that I needed $20,000 to help me get up. The lead Sherpa said,

"Get another guitar."

I said, "My grandfather carved that guitar himself from a tree that his grandfather had planted. The tree got struck by lightning every time it rained but did not fall, Tenzing. That tree stood there proud and tall, till he chopped it down."

Tenzing shrugged.

I handed over my life savings, which included the deed to my share of the farm, and one Wednesday morning we began to climb.

Thursday I felt ice vein and ice heart and chatter teeth.

Friday my left hand, my chord hand, crystallized.

Saturday it froze some more.

Sunday it was black.

On Monday morning I woke up with my hand gone and a fever spread over me. Tenzing passed me my hand. He'd cut it off to save my life.

Still we kept climbing.

Some of them turned back. I kept going. Most of them turned back. I climbed higher. One-handed but still going.

When I got to the top of the mountain, wouldn't you know, Dan Mayweather had left me a drawing in the snow. Two circles.

One with a smile. One with a frown.

I guess I was supposed to choose.

I journeyed down the mountain. And then the harder journey: home.

The farm was quiet. To my surprise no one came and took it away from me, even though it didn't belong to me any longer.

I cut crop circles in the corn for thirteen years.

Evie came to visit me once and said, "Do you play anymore?"

I held up my stump.

"Nope."

A black car came the next spring. The driver had a beard and a black hat and didn't look like he was from around here. Who is anymore?

He stepped out of the car and said my name, and I said "Yessir, that's me."

He said, "I'm sorry, boy. Dan Mayweather has left the Earth."

"So he's taken my guitar to Mars? That what you're saying?"

"No. He's passed away."

"Now I feel bad. We were fighting. He was my best friend. We came up together."

"Why were you fighting?"

"I don't remember."

"I understand."

The driver opened up the trunk and there was my guitar.

We were quiet for a while.

Contemplating life. And contemplating death. A songbird sang sorrowfully in a tree on the other side of the property. A tree I'd planted years ago that lightning wouldn't strike.

The driver sighed and said, "It's such a pretty guitar."

Well, don't you know, I picked the guitar up.

I held it high up in the air, admiring all sides of it. How it shone in the sun.

Then I smashed the guitar against my tractor. It burst into wooden shrapnel and strings flying everywhere like metal whips.

The driver jumped. Looked at me. Got in his car and made a wave of dust as he sped away.

There was a photo inside it that fell into the mud. A faded polaroid. The photo lay there in the splintered wood and the wet slop.

I picked it up with my aching fingers. Brushed all the crud off it.

Me and my friend. I was playing the guitar. He was sitting there next to me. How it usually was.

The back of the photo had a note that read: "All you was gonna do was sit there. Ever and ever and ever."

I slipped the photo into my back pocket.

I felt my missing hand make a phantom G chord.

I felt the hand move down the demolished neck of the vaporized guitar.

I felt the hand switch to an A7 chord.

And I—I began to strum.

Everyone (Everyone, Everyone, Everyone)

THE KID WITH SAD EYES SITS DOWN AND WRITES everybody an obituary. Haha. Everybody, including himself. Nobody's really dead. Well, his parents are. They're in the copper urn on the mantle.

He drains the last of his inheritance money to pay the fee. Then he clicks send. Then he throws the computer monitor out the open window so it crashes down into the garden. Ah, that feels so much better.

The next day everybody finds out. The paper has no news except those death notices. Everyone's friends and families, and enemies, and bosses and current lovers, and exes, too. Hmm, how do we feel about this?

The headline on the newspaper reads: RIP Y'ALL.

The first person to see it is a woman who's never taken a vacation. She wakes her husband. He's fine, he screams that the sun isn't even up. She slams a pillow down onto his face. He laughs. He's still breathing and pink and everything. And she checks her own pulse and sweet, still got it.

She races across town to the all-night 24/7 lawyer and skids into his office, "Hey, I wanna cash in an insurance policy."

She pulls her husband's obituary out of her pocket and shows the lawyer. The lawyer starts the paperwork, but gets buzzed by his secretary who says over the intercom that the bar has called, and he can't practice law anymore, he can only practice law in the cemetery—represent ghouls, goblins, and spirits stuck and stranded. The lawyer stamps his own forehead: rejected.

The woman comes home with no money and the husband is dressed in a Hawaiian shirt and a panama hat and she wails, "I'm so glad you're alive."

The husband and wife look out the window, and by now the word has spread. Everyone has something in common, finally.

So there is pandemonium. And there is euphoria. Everybody has arrived. Everybody is a goner. Nurses. Garbage men. Sex workers. Piano tuners. Dental hygienists. Bird watchers. Arsonists. Drunks. Mechanics. Florists. The angels and the devils of this material earth. Everyone is zero years old.

And so the church doors burst open and the nuns run naked through the street because there is no Heaven. They've been scammed. And the school children light the school house on fire and oh man, look at it burn, such a bouquet of color. And look, look, look, at the teachers running blind with ash all over their glasses. Running to the river to wash that no good knowledge off. And other things burn as well. The jail. The liquor store. The funeral home. And the firefighters don't care to save anything because deep down they never really wanted to be firefighters. So they smash out the bakery's plate glass window with their axes and steal the pies cooling on the racks. The firefighters mouths are full of huckleberry and key lime. They're eating cookies and donuts. And now they're sugar blind. And babbling like helpless children. And the police are gathered together, hiding in their secret cave, playing cards by candlelight, and planning for the aftermath of this apocalypse, and how they'll rebuild society so everyone left is a cop. And meanwhile, the mayor is floating away in a silver balloon with his face on it.

On the outskirts of town, a brother jumps in a window and has passionate sex with his sister's husband. The sister is healing herself out in the great wide open. On the outskirts of the outskirts of town, a little girl delivers a baby in the ink dark forest, birds whistling and dumb and unaffected as always. In the epicenter of wealth, the doctors and money men are dead and injecting heroin at home with their stereos up as loud as they can go. And the museum fills up with bloody handprints, each terror unique, and beautiful because it will never last. And the car dealership empties out because people come and simply say, "Hey I wanna test drive the gleaming fully loaded afterlife, lemme have—gimme gimme." No one can resist.

At this time the kid who wrote the obituaries wakes up in his room, and checks the internet and laughs in a panic for a second, and then he stops laughing. A bridge collapses. Nothing has been solved. He is cognizant of everything being ripped apart. He is still alone. Motherless. Fatherless. He flushes his phone down the toilet. He kicks in the TV. He whacks himself in the face with the biography of Albert Einstein.

He can hear his name being cursed. They've gathered in a mass in the shady yard. They know what he's done. They've come to eat his guts. He scrambles out his window and up onto the steep roof of his house. He pulls himself up to the peak and grabs hold of the weathervane. These people with their pitchforks and flaming torches. Basic bitches. It's the middle of the day. The house is a brick house and it can't be burnt. And nothing can be illuminated. The kid first tries to spit on all of them, but his spit won't get that far. The people try to set the lawn on fire but it won't.

The kid gets nervous and begins to tear shingles off the roof and launch them at the crowd. But then he has a solution. He pulls a white grease crayon from his pocket, and writes something on the shingle. He throws it down so it falls into the crowd. A sad old man bends down and picks up the shingle. "What is this?"

He yells, "A fucking blank birth certificate!"

The man's eyes light up. "Okay."

"Fill it out!"

A woman opens her purse. In lipstick, the person writes who they wanted to be. Nothing happens, at all, but the person is reborn. The kid watches the person walk off from the angry mob. Bounce in their step, headed towards the roiling destruction in every direction.

The remainder of the crowd is still worked up in a frenzy. They smash out the windows of the house. They break inside and turn on all the faucets, stuff the drains with the shirts off their backs, so the house quickly floods. They stomp up the stairs and he can hear them, ransacking his room and all he owns, and tearing up earlier drafts of the obituaries he wrote for their mothers and their fathers and their sons and their daughters and everyone else they loved.

The kid frantically tears off more shingles from the roof and fires the shingles down into the remaining crowd.

Each shingle is a blank birth certificate just like the ones before. Each person who catches one gets stars in their eyes about themselves.

Hooray I don't have to be me anymore.

Or, hooray, I liked myself, I can be myself again. I hereby declare myself officially whatever I want. Struck by lighting with goodness and thank you for your grace and mercy and benevolence.

Still, people crash through the ceiling in the hall and break into the attic and run out onto the roof where the kid is. A pig-tailed girl blind with rage shoves him off the roof. He falls down into the mass of people below. But their hands are up and they catch him.

And they carry him all through town, as he scribbles birth certificates on whatever he can find. Napkins. Underwear. Parking tickets. Priceless works of art, covered in shit and lying worthless and broken in the street.

By the time the sun is down, the fires have all burnt out, and the people are calm again and full of a dazed kind of unexamined faith.

The kid is set down in the sharp grass of the cemetery. And life seems to hold its breath, as if to solve an affliction of the hiccups. He relaxes and weeps at the ripe moon, rotting in outer space and dripping its joy and torture on the creatures below.

He weeps because he cannot not write new birth certificates for his parents whose urns have been knocked off the mantel and whose ashes have been dumped onto the rug by the intruders—those ashes washed out into the yard by a whoosh of water coming down the stairs.

Nothing can be done for true death. So he writes himself a new birth certificate. He becomes no one's son. No one's kin. No one's own.

He grieves them but stops belonging to them. He belongs to whoever else.

Maybe, belonging to everyone who is in the cemetery joining hands and singing a song with jumbled words and an uncertain future. These happy people caught in the breeze where their lives had been tilled, upheaved, shocked into motion from a standstill. These people standing on their feet now when maybe before they had crawled.

Oh no, please not them.

Sing sing sing, their song of hope that is this kid's new name. These people swaying back and forth and belting out the song of his new name. These people leaning in for a loving hug. Tears in their eyes and his new name on their lips.

And here he finally lifts his head and speaks—

Please shut up please shut up please can you shut the fuck up forever—when I catch my breath, I'll kill you all again.

The Wasteland Motel

HIS NAME WAS BO, FOR SOME REASON. I WAS writing this story, got lazy or whatever, couldn't think of a better name.

Bo was unhappy. He should've been grateful to be a member of one of the few clusters of humanity that had survived the apocalypse. Ah, whoop de doo.

One Wednesday morning he decided he wanted more from life, even if that meant danger. No more mind numbing safety, no more cowardly tending to the sheep: brushing them, feeding them slop, shoveling their shit. 32 years was enough.

He walked across camp and told Todd the sheep boss, "I'm putting in my two weeks notice."

Todd replied, baffled, "Your what?"

Nobody had heard of a two week notice. It was a cultural institution lost to time. A harborage of a past civilization that had gone belly up.

"I read about it in an old book that Crazy Charlie gave me when I was a kid ..."

Todd was still confused, he didn't know how to read, he barely knew what a book was. Charlie had been a lunatic, a drain on the camp, but he'd taught Bo to read. That was nice of him. Thanks Charlie.

Bo said it again, "Two weeks notice. I'm getting out of Dodge."

No one had ever quit a job post apocalyptically.

Todd said, "You're getting out of where?"

Everyone in camp was troubled by Bo's decision to leave. Especially Mort and Linda, who talked shit about Bo to whoever would listen. "He better not think he can waltz over here and get a job with us and our chickens ..."

"If he can't handle sheep, he certainly can't handle chickens."

"Or the eggs."

"Or the pecking."

They all agreed. They weren't hiring Bo. But Bo didn't come and ask anyone for a job. For his last two weeks there, he went about his business, conserving his water and rations, sharpening a spoon into a small dagger—his only defense against the unknown beyond the camp.

After his last shift with the sheep, he said goodbye to everyone. They'd gathered around in a loose circle, considering him nervously. Directly behind Bo was the rusty metal wall marking the forbidden perimeter. Nothing came in. Nothing went out.

"Where you going?" Clara asked.

"Into the Wasteland," Bo said offhandedly. "I'm trying my luck there."

The crowd drew a sharp breath. Maybe they thought this was all a joke. Nobody was really going out the gate.

Clara opened her mouth to say something but her mother kicked her shin. Clara said nothing else.

"This has been kinda fun," Bo said. "I'll come back and visit if you're not too sore about it all. I'm afraid I can't go on living this simple life." He had prepared a quote and he said it now, "As the philosopher Augustine of Hippo once said, The world is a book and those who do not travel read only one page."

"Book?" someone in the crowd murmured.

"Oh shit. Figures," said the mayor. He motioned to the guard, "Dave open 'er up. Let the kid go."

Maybe they should have all seen this coming. Bo was a strange dreamer. His dreams made the people in the camp have two distinct reactions. Some were afraid—people who dream can easily bring disaster. The rest of them were not afraid at all, just guilty because they weren't dreaming and felt they should, especially now that someone had dreamt to leave before they did.

"The Nukies are still out there. S'all I'll say, boy," a shriveled up old woman said. She was blind and could barely walk.

"Nukies, Jeez, it'd been a long time since somebody said that," the mayor remarked.

"Maybe there's werewolves out there too," Bo said, hoping to lighten the mood.

But it'd been so many years and people didn't know what to believe. The camp offered safety, but from what? Bo shook everyone's hand. The door was unlatched, with a great groan it was pried open for the first time in a generation. As he left, he said sincerely, "I hope to see you all soon."

"Don't forget the secret knock," the mayor said.

"Shave and a haircut, two bits," Bo said. With that he walked out into the desolate wastelands.

On the other side of the wall he began a new quote: "What is that feeling when you're driving away from people and they recede on the plain till you see their specks dispersing?"

The door was closed completely and latched now. He said this to the rusty wall: "It's the too-huge world vaulting us, and it's good-bye! But we lean forward to the next crazy venture beneath the skies!"

"That's beautiful," Clara's voice rang out, sounding very far away, even though it was just feet.

"Jack Kerouac."

It was a short walk, just long enough for him to contemplate what Crazy Charlie had told him many years ago, "Reason you suck at shoveling sheep shit is 'cause your family used to have a motel right up the road … You got motel owning in your blood."

"A what?"

"Motel," the old man said. "Fer vacationing. Very famous destination, people used to come for miles."

Charlie had stopped talking abruptly, looking at his knees. Before Bo could ask him what either a motel or vacation was, the old man freaking died. He stuck his tongue way out, it was swollen and grey. He fell over into the dust—dead.

The people in the camp were no help explaining what either thing were. Motel. Or vacation. "All Greek to me," Mort said.

The subject was dropped, but everyday for many years, Bo had wondered.

Bo crossed the mesa, surprised to see the new views of landscape opening up below him: an old paved road, a dilapidated white building with a large faded sign that said just MOTEL. He crouched and waited, looking all around at the sandy hills.

He didn't see any movement of any kind for a long while. The sun set and the moon came up. A smudged gold coin. Cautiously he went down from his lookout and entered into the motel.

Bo stayed there all alone, lonely and frightened. But after days and days of boredom, he put the worry out of his mind and occupied himself by straightening up the place (which looked like it had survived a nuclear war). He dug around in piles of paper, sorting through vast debris. It wasn't too long before he had a pretty good idea what a motel was supposed to be simply by reading brochures. He was stunned, gazing at old photographs, seeing an America many years before he was born, where people came and rested from the road, having gotten their fill of kicks on Route 66, they now relaxed, put their feet up and enjoyed an ice cold beverage. Wow. Imagine that? An ice cold beverage?

A week later, when Bo came back to the camp and explained about his new motel, they all laughed. He explained in detail what a vacation was. They laughed harder. "A wasteland vacation!" said Linda.

"No wonder you didn't want to shovel my sheep shit," the boss said. "You're a comedian, it turns out."

Bo was upset but still happy with his decision. He traded some goods discovered in the rubble for some much needed supplies. Then, he went back over the mesa, to his new home.

Early the next day, the first person arrived. Clara. She was a pretty girl. She didn't like the camp either. She'd decided she would sell her sex at the motel, something that she had been banned from doing in the camp, by Roger, the lone pain in the ass cop who had survived the apocalypse. At the motel she traded her body to Bo in exchange for room and board. Both were happy with the exchange. It was very professional. They shook hands afterwards.

He set her up in a room around the back. "Sorry about the giant concrete hole in the ground. When my funds get fluffier, I'll have it filled in. For now, be careful. Fall in, your brains will squish out your head." Clara looked down into the concrete hole, frowning.

With Clara there, a few men from town came to the Wasteland Motel, too. They visited with Clara and then sometimes stayed overnight in one of the rooms. Business wasn't great for Bo, but it was good enough. He filled the vending machine with orange sodas found in a storage room.

"I can add Continental breakfast soon if business keeps improving," he said.

One day, Bo found a set of keys. For what he had no clue. He showed Clara. She had no guess either. Bo regarded the keys curiously, setting them away. The mayor paid a surprising visit to the Wasteland Motel. He came on his dune buggy in a swirling haze of dust and noise.

Bo showed the mayor all around the grounds, proud of the amenities his motel had to offer. The mayor laughed. "Place is a dump." Then, Clara walked out onto the balcony and looked down on the men. She invited the mayor into her room. When he came out, he wasn't laughing. "I'm still not sure of this place," the mayor said. He got in his dune buggy and left. The next day, he came back with Mort's wife, Linda. He rented a room. He fucked her. Then Linda came and sat around in Bo's office and they shared a can of beef stew while the mayor went into the room with Clara again.

That day Bo found out what the keys were for. There was a hatch around back next to the big concrete hole in the ground. Bo unlocked the hatch and went down into the darkness. He was scared for his life but kept exploring. When he lit a match, he couldn't believe what he saw: stacks and stacks of white plastic bags. Inside the bags were chlorine pellets. He didn't know what chlorine was, but he figured it out rather quickly from the picture on the bag. The concrete hole in the ground was an empty swimming pool. How nice. Children in neon bathing suits were playing volleyball in the photograph.

There was another room down there too. Bo walked in and found many crates of red string. 4000 pounds of string. This too puzzled him, for some time—until the day that he found the large plaque buried under the rubble outside by the old broken road. The plaque said: The World's Second Largest Ball of String.

What a turn of events.

No one laughed at Bo anymore.

Eventually, the motel became a popular place for all the people from the camp. They came there to get away as time allowed with their work and they had goods available for trade.

On the one year anniversary Bo threw a big party at the motel. He invited the entire camp, free of charge. They opened the gate and all came over the mesa. It was a happy day.

They felt foolish about how afraid they'd been before, how much time they'd wasted cooped up like that. But now they were gathered around, joking, laughing, drinking, floating in the swimming pool. It felt good to dunk in the cool clear water and be out of the camp. They spoke about the odd curiosity of "The World's Second Largest Ball of String" and what it must have meant to travelers who saw it as they passed by in their fancy cars, when the road still went somewhere. But that was the other thing. "The road could still go somewhere, couldn't it?" Mort said.

"I suppose," the mayor admitted, floating on his back in the pool. The people began to smile, considering it—the nice thought of the world opening back up when it had seemed so destroyed and closed for so long. Bo looked up at the blue sky and felt the warm sun. He was proud that he'd left the camp, coming out there when everyone else had been so resistive and close-minded. Here they were all hopeful for the first time in many generations.

No one was worrying at all until the first shadows fell onto the pool. Deformed. Scab faced. Hairless humanoids. Mutants. They'd come out of their hiding spots in the hills and surrounded the motel armed with pickaxes, jagged hunks of rock, long sharpened strips of metal. Their eyes slowly wept blood. They were not concerned with "The World's Second Largest Ball of String," just the meat floating in the swimming pool.

The old blind woman in her pool float wheezed, "I told you so. I told you so. I told you so."

The pool turned a bright red. The bodies were torn apart. The

Nukie's ate. The night cooled down. The motel was left behind, again. The Nukie's dragged the remains of the bodies over the mesa, and through the unlocked, unguarded gate of the compound. Then they bolted the gate behind them, so that whatever was worse than them could not get into the compound in pursuit. The sheep cried in their pen at the sight of these new people. One of the Nukie's walked over, crouched down and stared at the sheep. With a voice like broken glass he finally spoke to the frightened sheep. He said, "Ssssh, it's alright. It's alright. We won't hurt you." The sheep got quiet, and began to believe.

Franklin

MY BROTHER ALMOST DROWNED IN AN INDUSTRIAL washing machine. The kind that lock from the front when you put your quarters in.

He had his own quarters, and gave them to a little girl in a powder blue jumpsuit. He was little himself. Nine, I think. Eight?

In the machine, he waved through the glass bubble, as she slammed the door.

The reason he didn't drown was because she ran away with his money and bought herself some candy at the store up the block.

Another time my brother came home soaked in diesel fuel. He'd held his nose and jumped off the hood of a dump truck, landed in an open 55 gallon drum of it behind the municipal garage. Lit match in hand.

This was that phase when he insisted I call him Human Torch, not Franklin, not Frankie, not Frank.

He didn't want to get in trouble. And I didn't want him to get in trouble either. So when he came to my window, reeking, I went out and helped him burn his clothes behind the trailer park, right there at the edge of the aqueduct where the coyotes howl.

When my brother shot himself, he was aiming for his heart. This was just last Christmas. Christmas Day and it was even snowing. Go figure.

He missed, thankfully, because thankfully he's stupid and doesn't know what side of his body his heart is on.

But I know.

And I'm still glad our parents were absent as much as they were, or else we would have been closely monitored. Taught things like right hand over left side of your body and face the flag.

In the room at the far end of the hallway, I can hear him wheeze my name through his busted lung.

And he is wild. And he has never had a chance.

And he does not know the Pledge of Allegiance.

When I Touch Your Face

THE WOMAN AT THE DESK HAS FRIZZLED HAIR AND sharp teeth. We're old friends.

"You don't have to sign in," she says.

She is smoking a cigarette in secret, her hand under the desk with the lit cigarette in it, the smoke drifting up, and her with this devilish smile on her face.

I wave and walk down that lemon and kelly green hallway.

On Thursdays for mandatory community service hours, I come here to read to the blind.

But like everyone else on this planet, the blind have no use for books.

Here are some of my lies:

I have lied about the Wizard of Oz. I gave him a hook for a hand and a fear of any kind of snake, big or small. I made the bricks out of watermelon sugar. I gave the witch heroin for blood. I had her speak in Nigerian Jazz.

I have re-fabricated other false pasts. Huckleberry Kim accidentally froze the Mississippi River, while her lover Tree Top Jim, swam in it. Kim used just a single drop of an experimental world destroying weapon called Ice Ice Baby Nineteen.

The Little Women all had flamethrowers, and could see the future by placing their palms on the foreheads of sleeping tigers. Jane Eyre died in a spelunking accident searching for El Dorado. Lot's Wife didn't turn to salt, she turned into a pterodactyl, which he rode with a sophisticated saddle, right into the center of a hole in the earth at the north pole, she lived happily ever after inside the earth, a place called Agartha.

You'd think I'd be more popular here.

But I'm not popular here.

The orderly won't look me in the eye.

He pretends to mop the floor as I pass, but my brain didn't melt in my fire. I know the bucket has no water.

My girl for today, the worst girl in the entire facility, is by the window.

She's maybe twenty years old. Maybe I am being punished by being given her.

Maybe she is being punished harder by being sentenced to me.

People like us are often herded together slowly by the invisible will of the damned, fake-happy.

I say, "Hello."

She looks. She has no pupils. Her eyes are solid milk.

"Ah you!"

She springs from her wheelchair—onto sure legs, surprises me.

"You don't need that, I guess."

"Oh me? I'm a back flipper from way back."

With her palms, she smooths the creases of a dress overrun with goldfinches.

Maybe she is at an eighth grade mixer waiting to be asked to dance, but is feral and just got done foaming at the mouth through the braces. I have no corsage. My parole officer wants me to take a job at the municipal dump: night shift.

"You can tell a lot of things about a person from their hand shake," she says.

Her hands are like burnt ice cream.

"What does mine say?"

"You were in a fire," she grins.

I sit down on the bed. "Yeah, I was in a fire, Nancy Drew."

She sits back down in her wheelchair, proud of herself. Probably somebody else in the home told her about me already. They're kicking field goals with me here.

The blind have no love for me either.

"How'd the fire happen?"

"Ah shit, shut up."

"I wanna know—tell."

"Why you roll around in a wheelchair if you don't need it?"

"I like to bump into things. I want a demolition derby. I've listened to them on TV. They sound fun. I'm tired of feeling around. How'd you get cooked?"

"Oh it was stupid. I was trying to set my motorcycle on fire. I was trying to blow it up. For the insurance money."

"What's it like to ride a motorcycle?"

"I'd feel bad describing it."

"Probably feels like being a loud bird, I'd guess."

"Loud bird. Yes, that's it."

"Low flying monster hawk."

I've got Life of Pi on the coffee table. I am trying to decide if I am going to make the tiger be the entire forces of Nazi Germany or if I am going to make the boat be a kite.

"Did you hurt anyone else, burning the bike?"

"Just me."

"Do you want to feel my face?" I ask.

"No, that's okay."

"Don't you want to know what I look like?"

"I can tell from your voice and the things you say that you're ugly, but don't take that the wrong way. It's the tone of your voice."

I laugh. She's right. I say, "You're no looker either."

"We make a good pair, an asshole and a blind girl."

"Well, you're not just blind, you're also an asshole. I don't think I'm gonna read to you."

"Oh boo hoo. You sound like you're from New Jersey. People from New Jersey don't even know the whole alphabet."

"Where you from?"

"I'm from Hell."

She stands from the wheelchair and walks over. "I changed my mind, let me feel your face."

"Nah, get away from me."

"Don't be a pussy," she whispers.

I look over my shoulder and the orderly is looking in the doorway and suddenly I'm more paranoid about looking like a punk who's afraid of a little girl, so I give in.

I stare at her blank eyes as she runs her fingers across the rippled folds of my cheek, my brow, my chin, my twisted nose.

"You were foolish," she says.

"I've heard that."

"You don't even have glasses on. Do you wear contact lenses?"

"No."

"20/20 vision."

She smiles again. Her teeth are perfect but for some reason still have metal braces.

"I want to show you what I see, sometimes it's better than a dream."

"What do the blind dream of?"

"Shhhh."

I let her close my eyelids for me.

I let my lids fall. Let them seal in total.

"Don't get nervous. Just relax."

"I'm relaxed."

She rests her fingers on my eyeballs, applies slight pressure.

And then the world lowers its volume. The world hums and says goodbye rappelling down a deep chasm. The sky folds in and the clouds fold in, all vacuumed away into a chamber of perfect snow packed nothing.

This must be why people meditate or do the dishes.

She applies greater pressure.

With the pressure I can see my blood vessels.

I see a faint purple light rising.

Then a pink.

The light becomes brighter. It transitions to orange and then white and then back to pink.

She presses slightly harder.

I sigh, completely gone gone.

"Here it comes," she says.

"What?" I say, hoping to be shown a vine obscured temple, a white lightning sneezing horse, a volcano of pinball answers, a question that erases itself. The music, perhaps, of my life, I've never heard, but have often longed for.

But instead—

This is when she rips my eyelashes off.

"Are you fucking kidding me!"

The orderly comes through the door and pushes her back in her wheelchair.

She's celebrating like she just kicked the winning field goal and I am the Super Bowl.

And I'm walking down the hallway with my hand over my face, just a little blood, but oh god the pain and the orderly is saying, "You okay, man? You okay?"

"I'm peachy."

"I knew she was gonna do that shit."

"Thanks for the heads up."

"Anytime," he says, slapping my back.

The woman at the desk has finished her secret cigarette. She smiles the smile of a deeply embedded spy, "They love you here."

I'm all temporary hate.

She signs my paperwork.

I glance at the two more community service hours added to my tally. And I think about how I could have stayed picking up trash on the side of the road. Or I could be washing and waxing cars at the police station. Or I could be giving out soup at the shelter.

"You coming back?" she asks.

A drop of blood from my face, lands on her hand, the slip, the metallic butcher block desk.

I say, "Everyone is hurt—everyone is angry. I'm right at home."

"Bout sums it up," she says, passing my slip to me.

4

Rabbit Driving Cellphone

EVERYONE'S ON THEIR PHONES. I MEAN OUT IN THE world. And also here's a drawing of a rabbit driving a car and he's talking on his cellphone and it even looks like a stick shift. Can you drive stick shift?

I was driving when my friend texted me and the text said: 'Hey can you believe that I just saw a baby in a stroller texting someone. Who could that baby possibly be texting?'

I wrote back: 'Other babies in other strollers with cell phones.'

If you look closer, the car isn't even a car. It's a drawing of a cellphone and everyone is riding on the cellphone and propelling forward at like crazy warp speed, clouds coming out of the tailpipe. You know how fast you have to be going to create enough moisture to make a cloud?

Look it up on your cellphone.

I was thinking about how long it's been since I felt lost, and it's got to be like 2008. I haven't been lost since 2008. Since my first smarty pants phone. We all have instant maps in our pockets now and if you're not sure where you are, you can at least see that you're alive and you're a glowing blue dot on an LED screen that repositions by way of satellite.

See that, even satellites are into what you do.

Here's a drawing of a pig taking a selfie.

Think of that the next time you're taking a selfie. Think of cartoon swine. Think of yourself as cartoon swine.

Here's a drawing of a dog in a pair of Levi's hunched over in a fetal position gazing into its cellphone screen. Think about how happy dogs usually look in cars. How they are jumping up and down and staring out a window. And how much they love the driver and the other passengers. Well, no love here, everyone is on their phones.

And here's a drawing of a book worm with no books to worm anymore. He's proofreading his own death certificate via eBook app, yeah buddy.

My father didn't have a lot of money. A good 25% of my youth was spent driving around from strip mall to strip mall in NJ, price shopping, comparing the cost of a certain toaster at this store and then driving to the next store and telling the toaster salesman in store #2, "I'M NOT PAYING THAT, STORE #1 HAS THAT TOASTER FOR A DOLLAR LESS."

Now there are no salesmen. They're on their cellphones. At home. Unemployed. And there are no stores, you are buying that toaster from your car, as you drive, on your cellphone.

Even right now you're reading this on your cellphone, most likely, hiding out in the shadows at work, or sitting in a chair somewhere waiting for the moon or a loved one or your birthday.

You're that drawing of the cellphone on their cellphone riding on the cellphone as it speeds along, and you, you've got your sunglasses on, because you're hiding from the real world, and it's bright in the glowing world you prefer, the one you keep in your pocket.

5

Only the Gentle

MY FATHER WAS AN AUTODIDACT. HE CUT HIS OWN hair without a mirror. Good, too.

He was also a self-taught criminal who liked broad-daylight-breaking-and-enterings; slips, falls; tumbles in the minor rough; squeaky supermarket scams.

The crimes got worse as I got older.

A bogus check for my 7th birthday with Clarabell Simpkin's name forged on it.

A disassembled revolver found in his spare boots when I was ten.

My freshman year of high school, fires were lit in the dark making money rain from the branches of well-insured trees. I was able to get a drum set.

Mom left. Well, I mean, Mom changed the locks.

One snowy afternoon, during his visitation, we took a foggy bus three towns over to his new place.

He pointed at a little brick house and said, "Run inside and grab the salt and pepper shakers off the table, I'll wait here. Want to show you something."

I refused, suspecting it wasn't his house.

And I was right.

Later, same day, he taught me how to drive stick shift in a stolen Chevy rack body.

Joke was, "If you can get good at this, you can be my getaway driver."

Other joke was, I did want to get away.

Once, I found a photocopy of my father hanging up in the post office and so for Christmas I bought him a shaving kit and a pair of spectacles without a prescription lens. If it could work for Superman, it could work for my father.

When he got the job as a stuntman on the movie set, he said he was finally straight.

Crime hadn't freed him. His hair was long now, down past his shoulders.

He liked the sense of adventure on the film set, the risk, the cash, invisibility in a different way.

Sometimes Mom would go to the backlot for snacks and soda at the craft service table. As far as I know, that was the extent of her alimony.

I think she was just trying to catch a glimpse of a movie star, or maybe have one notice her.

But that's life.

Mom bloomed. She went on a date with the milkman. She went on a date with a cop. Then another cop. A firefighter came to Easter dinner.

On the TV, I saw my dad fall out of a window fifty stories up. He free fell towards safety.

And no longer did I have to settle into my predestination as a mere accomplice. I was materializing. I brushed my teeth through a grin. The university applications went out en masse. Not a single response came to our crooked mailbox.

I straightened it in superstition.

Still nothing.

I held my breath as the bus thundered past the cemeteries of my grimy hometown. I lifted my feet crossing every train track junction.

My guidance counselor said five Hail Mary's, punctuating it with a shot, "You won't need to worry about loans if you're an ace safe cracker."

But I had tossed my stethoscope into the ocean on a trip with my mother to the coast for her birthday. A gray day. We ate cotton candy and she told me about the first time dad had brought her a gift. One thousand red roses filled up the entire bed of a pickup truck belonging to who knows.

It was love right away.

One rainy night Dad showed up to Mom's house in a red hatchback I'd never seen, flames and skulls on the side. "Stunt car," he said. "Borrowed it. Let's go."

I thought he meant, go and keep driving and never come back.

But he added these instructions, "Drive us to the Parkerstown Bridge."

It was almost midnight. I had school in the morning.

As I drove, the lights flashed across his face and I saw his teeth for the first time. Mouth vulnerable. His nose looked fake. Same with the chin. Who was this guy?

We got out and stood on the bridge. Leaned over the railing. Looked down at the water—the river rushing away from us.

"Heard you got accepted to a school," he said.

"News to me," I said, stunned.

"Intercepted this the other day …"

He held up an envelope that looked like it'd been ripped apart, burnt, then reassembled with scotch tape.

The letter inside said I was taken by my top university. Way on the other side of the county.

"Probably won't see you again," he said.

Figured he was right, so I shrugged.

"Help me with a job before you leave."

He pointed to the hatchback. I followed him over and we popped the hatchback.

Inside was a black bag. Oblong. Lumpy.

"What's that?"

"A dead body," he said. "Have to throw it in the river but it's too heavy. Need your help. Big strong youthful brawn." He unzipped the bag and I could see a man with blood caked over his face. The eyes were wide and like the surface of the moon.

"Will you help me?"

I didn't hesitate. I grabbed one end of the bag and he grabbed the other end of the bag and with all our strength we hoisted the body over the railing of the Parkerstown Bridge.

I watched the bag slap the water. I watched the dead man float out of it.

My father grabbed my shoulder and kissed me on the ear so hard it rang for days.

"I'm so goddamn proud of you."

It was the first time he said that. It made me feel so loved, that all I wanted to do was commit crimes with my old man, go from bank to bank, go from murder to murder, be together. Torch houses, collect insurance moola. Boost tractor trailers. Hijack planes. Blow up buildings. Run.

I felt a tear rolling down my face. I lowered my head, embarrassed.

I looked again at the water below. There was a problem.

"Hey Dad …"

"What?"

"The body isn't sinking …"

"It won't," he said, "It's fake. Got it from the set."

"Oh."

"Dummy."

I looked at him with rage.

"Polypropylene."

We got back in the hatchback, he took me home.

My father was coated in a chemical jelly, lit on fire by the stunt coordinator, urged into a beautifully choreographed jog that would be fixed to proper speed in post.

He moved gracefully—arms pumping, head up, chin up—pushing down an artificially-happy-nuclear-family street on backlot number 9.

The cheers of the extras, paid just fifty dollars each for the day and given sandwiches, were his true family.

Manufactured onlookers who loved him.

Save for one, my mother, at the catered booth sinking her teeth into a bagel with hot pink lox.

"Quiet on the set!" the assistant yelled. Into the bullhorn the director said, "Action!"

Off I went to college.
My father moved into my old room.
He began cutting his own hair again, and then hers.
The firefighters went back to the firehouse.
The cops went back to the station.
The prop body we tossed off the Parkerstown Bridge was pulled out to sea, a small island, adrift.

Temporarily Here

HE TURNS THE RADIO DOWN. SHE TURNS THE RADIO up.

"Don't mess with the dial, I'm driving."

A car cuts her off. She lays on the horn and speeds up. Almost wrecks.

"Yo! What're you doing?" Bob says.

"I'm driving, shut the fuck up."

They've been fighting all morning. He turns the radio dial down, she slaps his hand. The light turns green, the car jets forward.

"Yeah, pull over, I'm out of here."

The baby girl cries in the baby seat.

"Bitch pull over."

"Get a life, I'm not pulling over."

They're in the far right lane and she's not slowing. He opens the door and jumps out of the car.

He crashes down, but rolls to his feet.

She keeps driving, baby girl crying, radio up. There's a parking lot as big as a small country. He walks through it.

The bar is slow. It's early afternoon. Kyle sits alone. The bartender is eating Chinese food on the wrong side of the bar.

Bob says, "I want your tallest and strongest drink." But he's bleeding severely from his head and doesn't know it.

"Can't serve you. Get going." The bartender points to the door.

Kyle stands up, "Robbie?"

"Oh hey, man." It's a coincidence, they haven't seen each other since high school.

"You're bleeding on the floor. Get out or I call the cops."

Kyle says, "No! He's with me, bro. He's cool." Ultimately though, they're both not getting served now. Bartender crosses his arms and everything. Kyle grabs his car keys and says to Bob, "Let's get out of here, this place is lame."

They're in his Pontiac and pulling out of the parking lot, back onto the highway when Kyle finally says, "So how'd you get all mangled up?"

"Jumped out of my wife's car."

"Whoa. That's intense. Trouble in paradise?"

"She's a psycho."

"She's so crazy you jumped from a moving—oh, hold on—" Kyle stops the car in traffic, rolls his window down, vomits.

Cars zip around the stopped Pontiac, horns sounding off.

"You better move!"

Kyle rolls the window up, puts the car into gear.

There're breath mints in the ashtray, which isn't used as an ashtray.

"Sorry, got rained out at work today."

Bob looks up at the infinite blue sky.

They park behind the Food Universe. Two reasons for that. Kyle has to piss and there's a picnic table under a shady tree next to the cardboard dumpster. Kyle has a car bar. His trunk has fifths of bourbon, rum, vodka, and even pilsners on ice in an Igloo cooler.

They sit at the picnic table and relax.

"Where are you supposed to be?"

"Mother-in-law's house. This is better."

"What's happening there?"

"Birthday party."

Kyle hands Bob a large leaf from an oak tree. Bob sticks the leaf on his head where the blood is trickling out. It works.

They're both drinking now from the fifth of rum, passing it. And the air is cool behind the supermarket. And it feels like another world. The meadow is full of chirping birds and Bob says, "I can't remember the last time I heard birds chirp."

"Sometimes it's the only joy I get."

Bob remembers something, knows he shouldn't mention it, but it's already on the tip of his tongue so he just says it, "I watched Greg Pollock kick your ass in front of the school bus that day and I didn't do anything about it."

"Oh that's a painful memory."

"Sorry to bring it up. You were bleeding from your head. Worse than this."

"Know why he did that?" Kyle says.

"I heard some things."

"Because I like boys. I'm a fag, as they say."

"Well, fuck," Bob says.

Kyle shrugged. "Nobody leaves anybody alone."

"My dad would have shot me, though."

"Your dad wouldn't have shot you."

"My dad would have though, for real. He did shoot me once." Bob pulls his shirt sleeve up and shows where the bullet went through his bicep. There was a scar on the tricep where it exited.

"For what? Why'd he shoot you?"

"When he was teaching me how to drive, he ditched me in the middle of nowhere. I came home with the car empty. Didn't put gas in it."

"Wow, that's extreme."

"He drove me way out into the woods, must have driven down trails for three hours. Finally he stopped. There was another pickup truck there waiting. A friend of his. Dad said goodbye, climbed in the truck and said, 'If you can find your way home you're a man.'"

"People can be assholes."

"I heard Greg Pollock got blown up in a desert."

"Cheers."

Kyle kills the last of the rum and says, "Well I gotta go inside and stock motherfucking cat food. This was fun. Let's do this again sometime, yeah?"

"Sure. You work there? Didn't know."

"Life is a hell of a bright room but has curtains that work."

He gives Bob some iced down beers, slips on his Food Universe smock and walks off with a wave.

Bob walks down the shoulder of the highway again. The blood has thinned. He wipes it with his shirt sleeve and now he looks like a murderer just moseying along.

A police car stops. Two female cops step out.

"Where are you coming from?"

"Haha, still coming out of the woods."

One of the officers, Pam, recognizes Bob from high school and she says hi.

"Oh hi, Pam. This is all my own blood."

"It's cool," she says. "You want to get in the car?" She opens the back of the squad car. Bob climbs in without resisting.

"What happened?" The lead officer says.

"Jumped out of a moving car."

"Want to go to the hospital?"

Pam opens the medical kit in the glove box. She passes back some gauze through the partition.

"I'd like to just go home if that's okay."

"Pass your ID up. Gotta run it first to see if you're a wanted man. Then, sure. No problem. Home."

Bob looks out the window. Nothing to see. Strip Mall, America.

"Saw Kyle Yearling today," he says. "Remember him?"

"Oh" Pam says. "Of course, Prom King."

"He's doing pretty good."

"Glad to hear it."

"Zen optimist cat food happy drunk."

"Excellent."

Bob's cell phone rings. It's his daughter. Baby girl.

"Daddy where are you?"

"Cop car."

"Another car? I'm confused. Why'd you jump out of our car?"

"Sometimes people just make mistakes."

"Yeah."

"Remember yesterday when you threw your PBJ on the floor."

"Yeah."

"What'd I do?"

"You picked it up."

"Yup, picked it up and I made you a new sandwich and then I ate the one you threw on the floor."

"Yeah."

"You know why I did that?"

"Because you love me."

"I do."

"You and mommy going to get a divorce?"

"No. No we aren't."

"Good. Daddy, I have to go, the cake just came out. Bye."

"Bye."

Pam hands the ID back. "Off we go, you're good."

Bob leans against the glass. "Want to take me to a birthday party instead?"

"Would we have to bring a gift?" Pam asks.

"No gift."

"Let's go."

Forks, Knives, Spoons

THERE IS A SMALL GAP BETWEEN THE KITCHEN SINK and the wall. I've dropped, over time, all our forks down there. They cannot be retrieved. We eat with our hands now. Sometimes I sneak out on the fire escape, and climb up two stories to catch my ex-wife at her desk. She must be aware of me out there; there's something backwards-romantic as she slips photographs of our wedding day into a can of neon paint, obliterating our memories. She hangs them to drip dry on a series of clotheslines in the room. Later, the neon photos are completed with fine line depictions of animals, places, men, wars, music, all better than me. I'm fine with that.

Sam scoops palm-fulls of oatmeal, it's his new method. He's straight-faced.

I say, "We have spoons, you weirdo."

"But for how much longer?" he says.

Josh wants me to know, "Saw your Berlin jogging yesterday, she looked good."

"You know we aren't married anymore."

"Oh? Saw her running down Cabrini Boulevard in her wedding dress. I honked."

"Performance art," I assure him. "One more thing, rent is due."

Tim doesn't have rent either. But he finds a box turtle I never see poke his/her head out of the shell. He brings it home, and the three of us sit on the floor, staring at the turtle.

"Brightens up the place."

"Was in the middle of the road."

"Doing what?" I ask.

"Just sitting there. Frozen. Maybe it gave up."

"Suicide," I say.

We all look towards the bathroom.

"Sam's been in there for two hours now."

"Guy loves that bathtub."

I've tried many tactics: magnets, duct tape and wire, a broom handle, even going so far as to inquire how to shut the water off beneath the sink and move the entire unit. None of my attempts have been successful. One night I have a dream that the last butter knife is down there too. I am completely alone, in an apocalyptic wasteland, and I cannot even put butter on toast. Well, we don't have a toaster anyway, but that's beside the point.

Josh moves out abruptly. He leaves a note with a few reasons:

"#1 I'd like to have access to a bathtub.

#2 Where is the vegetable peeler my mother sent me? And the beer bottle opener(s).

#3 That turtle freaks me out. A bad omen.

#4 The internet here is slow."

He ends the note saying, "In all seriousness, I think I'm going to move to the sewer."

Tim goes on a date, but is weird about it. Then he goes on a another date and is weird about that too. Then he says, "I think I'm in love but it's complicated." Then he goes to meet with her family. After, he inquires about the vacant room, "I'd like my new girlfriend to move in." We vote as a house. House vote is, "Sure."

When the new girlfriend shows up, I'm worried. She has no books in her many cardboard boxes. She won't look us in the eye. She is intensely private. She stays in her room, never comes out. In the night, she softly plays a violin, that I cannot find, no matter how often I search her room. The most troubling part, and the reason of course that Tim said 'it's complicated,' is she has her own silverware, washes it by the window, does not ever carry it beyond the threshold of her own door.

Berlin burns the wedding dress in the square. It's filmed. The film is eventually screened. I'm invited. I go. We kiss furiously. Berlin moves into my room, for a time. That doesn't last, I move into her room for a time. That doesn't last either, our problems are the same. We go back to just being neighbors.

One afternoon, I take the box turtle upstairs to her apartment. We place the turtle on a tarp, and make small pools of paint all around the turtle. With his/her head still hidden, he/she begins to walk around through the paint. "It doesn't even look where it goes."

"But look how beautiful it's gotten."

"What? The painting or the turtle?"

Sam dies in the bathtub. Even Josh comes to the wake. Tim wears Sam's other suit and holds the many-colored turtle. His new girlfriend stays home in her room, and I assume, plays the violin. Afterwards, we go to the corner bar and Josh tells us how nice the sewers are. I'm distracted. On the wall, of course, are all the photos that used to be from my wedding day. I point to an orange one with Ella Fitzgerald drawn in fine geometric lines.

"That's a beautiful one."

"Look how happy we were," Berlin says.

My wedding ring is down there. Her wedding ring is down there. Two cellphones are down there. My car keys are down there. Four hundred cumulative forks, knives and spoons are down there. Countless kitchen gadgets are down there. A notebook with half a novel slipped down there.

There, there.

Roast Beast

SHE SENT ME THIS YOUTUBE VIDEO OF A CAT trapped in a house. The cat should be meowing/hissing, but instead somebody dubbed themselves going "heyyyyyyyy" every time it opens its mouth.

I watched the video for awhile, getting to the end and then restarting from the beginning.

Outside the window, the sun climbed the sky and set all the puffy white clouds on fire so they fell in the river, sizzling. Think this was Thursday.

The couch hurt so I got off it and walked to the trash can where she'd thrown away my flip flops, for some reason. I put them on.

I wanted a roast beast sandwich from the Uzbek deli on the corner by the fire house so I began this great journey off my couch, leaving the crumbling apartment, and joining the bubbling world.

Oh look at this. Outside the building, there were purple flowers at the bottom of the staircase in a massive concrete cauldron that had always been empty, that I assumed the founders of this city had used to boil heretics alive. Okay, now it has purple flowers. Cool.

Out of a doorway by the abandoned Lutheran church, a man

stumbled onto the sidewalk behind me.

He looked like a zombie, minus the gore, but also in green flip flops.

Earlier today one of my friends posted this on Twitter: "Where can I score the super mega heroin, the kind that makes 2016 die forever?"

I @'d the friend, "If you are serious about the super heroin, you can get it at the abandoned Lutheran Church by my apartment."

You can get blocked for even the slightest helpful thing.

I dm'd the friend on a different platform.

I turned back and snapped a picture of the church on my cellphone and tagged the friend on Instagram.

"You taking my picture?" the flip flop zombie said.

"Heyyyyyy," I said to the flip flop zombie. But the flip flop zombie didn't say anything else.

The sun was killing us on that side of the street, so without discussing it, we both crossed the street into the shade of the women's Catholic college, its big brick facade and angels up there on the roof with machine guns. I felt like I was in a slow motion flip flop chase scene, and so I laughed and laughed.

But the joy began to wear off halfway to the firehouse. The guy's flip flops were loud as hell, as if amplified. Flop flap flop flap.

I walked faster and my feet too, went flop flap flop flap.

In front of the luxury condominiums, the guy walked through a puddle made by a broken sprinkler, and his flip flops got even louder and wetter. Sucking and squishing. Fllweep flawwp flawwp vluuurt flerrrp.

I pulled over and let the guy get ahead of me so I wouldn't have to listen anymore.

The back of his t-shirt said: If Life Gives You Lemons, Obviously, Just Have Sex With The Lemons.

He vanished around the corner, and was never seen again.

I walked the rest of the way to the Uzbek deli, and just so you know, there is no one from Uzbekistan that works there and they don't make or sell any Uzbek food.

The ebb and flow of change is too swift for any business around here to keep up with on something as temporarily permanent as their own sign.

As I opened the door, the clerk killed the music, 90s hip hop. After a pause where he looked me over and contemplated me, he pushed a button and rockabilly music bursts from the stereo. Reverb drums and walking bass line and sunshine guitar. Hiccup vocals.

"I'm not rockabilly, bro," I said.

But the way he looked at me, I knew that truly, in the eyes of the world, I was rockabilly and there was nothing I could do to stop it.

White t-shirts here on out. Pomade and indigo Levis. Converse sneakers. These flip flops are going back in the trash.

I ordered the roast beast sandwich. The sandwich was three dollars more than it used to be because of the luxury condominiums, but I was up against a wall. I Yelped the place with two stars complaining about the three dollar increase and there was nothing more I could do. My powers began and ended at Yelp.

While I waited for my suddenly fancy sandwich, my phone buzzed and it was her again.

She found another video, a kitten escaping out of its pen by scaling an impossible glass wall, and then hopping into a different pen with an alligator, but the alligator is asleep.

The kitten crawls across the alligator's snout. Dark scales with flecks of bright green.

And one eye of the alligator opens. An eye like a ripe lemon with a black exclamation point for a pupil.

And then the alligator raises its jaw, slowly and methodically, a drawbridge opening with a car on it … and so like this, the kitten doesn't even notice what is happening.

But the kitten is curious, and leans over the nostrils and hanging on to the edge, shivering, it peeks into the tunnel full of jagged teeth and sinister hot breath.

And the alligator seems to smile as it benignly wheezes, "Heyyyyyyyyyyyyyyyyyyyyyy."

Double Bird

FIRST WARM NIGHT, I PRY OPEN MY WINDOW.

Who nailed this shut?

The room is dark. The apartment quiet. Today I took a seven hour bath, but kept the drain slightly open and the hot water dripping.

Hour six of that bath: I gained sudden love for this wayward human race.

I remembered a magazine article that said there is a 40 million to 1 chance of ever being born.

After all that struggle, you'd think we'd be kinder to each other once we're here.

Tonight, finally the radiators are silent.

Finally, I've forgiven everyone who's trespassed against me.

There is no traffic outside. The highway wrapping around this city is vacant. Birds have not come back yet.

Bugs either. Or the ice cream man.

But there is the swiss cheese moon, and I wave at it, pushing my duck feather pillow away, rolling over. Maybe I'll never sleep again. Just stay up, make Erfff better. Make grass and dirt better.

City is better.

Heart heart, big building, walls that push out or suck in with the breath of a communal zillion, all lottery winners by getting born.

The dirt road I grew up on had no art, no magic Chinese herbs or acupuncture, no ballet, no police chasing crooks across rooftops, bounding building to building; no sorcery; no opera sung in warped hallways; no weeping in stairwells—certainly had no great heights.

I hope I see some of that soon.

Have gotten bored and have taken it out on my arch nemesis in this neighborhood—lives across the street. I squint at his dark window.

I have every modern convenience, including this zippo lighter. Namaste.

Light a cigarette in bed.

Sigh. Raise screen, hang head out over street.

Goddamn, what is that?

A shriek.

Across the street, a shriek like an eagle falling out of a sky it once owned.

Red hot firework coming at me …

Goddamn!

Jump out of way of rocket and sparks kissing my bearded cheek. My cigarette falling in bed.

The Roman Candle bounces off the closet door, ends up in my laundry hamper full of dirty clothes.

I shout, "Fuck! Fuck!"

I spring up, "Fuck. Fuck."

Sprint to kitchen. Stub toe on door jamb. Hamper clothes on fire. Open cabinet door—grab the fire extinguisher and run back into room—fuck fuck—flickering firelight and hurry—remove fire fighting pin! And depress handle! And a putter of wind but no powder comes out of the extinguisher.

Toe broken. Toe bleeding.

I run back into the kitchen and grab the spaghetti pot off the stove—fill it with water, onto the spaghetti that is left in the pot and toss that on the fire—smoke detector screaming and I'm panting like an animal.

But, great whoooooosh and fire done.

Clothing ruined. Charred.

Popping, spitting, steam and smoke.

Then I'm back at window coughing, looking out.

And now orange light across street.

His bedroom light on.

The kid is sitting in the window.

Bandages wrapped around his skull from where I hit him in the head yesterday with a jug of rotten leftover milk.

"Well played you little shit!"

He waves the middle finger at me.

I cross and uncross double birds at him, arms weaving in and out.

"Even?" I shout.

"Hell no, old man."

Smiling.

Slamming our mutual windows down.

Both smiling.

I see my favorite pillow burning up from the cigarette; I grab the cigarette, stick it in my teeth. Pat the fire out with my palms.

And there on my bed sheet is a single ant, crawling out from whatever winter was.

There on the sheet, the first of many ants crawls out from whatever winter was.

Blue, Blue, Electric Blue

THERE'S A CALLER ON THE RADIO SHOW WHO TELLS a story about the time he left his red Ford Escort in a parking lot, and when he comes out of the store, his car is gone.

"I specifically remembered where I'd left it, because I like to park close to the cart corral. But when I came out, it wasn't there. It was parked all the way over by the entrance to the garden center."

"So what do you think happened?" the host asks.

"I have no idea," the caller says.

That's how I feel sometimes. That's how I wound up in here. I keep lifting the mattress and looking for myself. I keep searching the carpet. I search the electric blue walls for any kind of clue. I'm like the man who walked out of the store with a plastic bag full of nuts and bolts and can't figure out why his car is parked over by the garden center.

May comes in, sits in the chair by the window like we're old friends and she didn't take away my cassette tapes when I came in here and like she didn't make me write this stuff in this notebook that they take and read every night. Have a seat May. The radio show is over anyway. They're playing a loud advertisement for a drag race happening this Sunday. Sunday! Sunday! Kids Free! May flicks the power off. She's the kind of person who could never turn anything on. But boy o boy, look at her flick things off.

"Wanna tell you what was happening."

"When?" she says, pushing record on her handheld device.

I point at the transistor radio.

"Missing in action. Was gonna tell you about the missing in action story on the radio. But instead I'll tell you how I lost my first car, related story, kinda."

"How'd you lose your car?"

"I didn't sleep for three weeks. And then I figured out why."

"Why?" She's been waiting to hear this story since I showed up here.

"World was ending of course," I say. "Problem was I was the only one who knew. So you know what I did? I emptied my bank account, gave it out to friends. Bet they were happy. It was cold out. January. But I knew I had to drive my car to God, and I also knew that I couldn't get to God in my car if I had clothes on, so I threw them in the trash outside Fried Paradise and I got in my car and I hit the gas. I hit it hard."

"Where were you driving?"

"The water. Barnaget Bay. Sun was setting on the bay and the bay was frozen and the ice looked like it was on fire and like God was out there standing on the ice."

"Did you meet Him. Or Her. Or It?"

"No, didn't make it." I get quiet.

"What happened?"

"Crashed my car into a dune where the boardwalk ended. Totaled it. Sun went down. Never got to meet Him or Her or It. Just went for a walk, naked and freezing to death down the boardwalk."

"World still ending?"

I open my mouth to say something, but I swear, there is a crash outside the window. May jumps up from her chair and leans against the chicken wire glass.

"O No!" she says.

There is a baby blue Volkswagen bent around a pine tree. The door flies open. I watch Gerry Nowhere run into the brush, barefoot and in his white gown with the tiny orange starbursts.

The fat security guard runs into the woods a minute later. I'm still waiting to hear Gerry's side of the story.

The other side of the story that I hear is that this guy Justin, who is so nice and kind and brings soggy stinking silverfish paperback books donated through the St. Barnegas Catholic Church, well the Volkswagen is his car, or was his car before Gerry Nowhere got in it. The car was left running while Justin carried boxes of donation books in. Well, look at that, no good deed goes unpunished. Can't drive a car towards God or away from him, I guess.

When May makes a move to run out of the room, I block her with my body and I say, "Hey wait a minute."

"No, please move."

"So the caller couldn't find his car, and the host says, 'Any idea how your car could have moved?'"

"You're not making any sense." She yells for help, but all the help is out in the front of the convalescent home, looking at the crashed car.

I put my hand on her shoulder and I lead her back into the chair by the window.

And I say, "The host thought that some other shopper came out with a similar key. That maybe some other shopper walked the wrong way and saw this red Ford Escort and thought it was theirs and when they climbed in and tried the key, it worked, because sometimes things just work. When the guy who lost his car found his car by the garden center, the CD player was on. It was going off like a bomb, at top volume. Person had it wrong, but they were able to drive themselves back to where they needed to go, nobody had to get involved. Self correction. Parked the wrong car next to the right car, went back on with life."

"Okay, I understand. I understand," she says.

And I let her out of the room.

And now my radio is gone.

And now it's just this notebook.

What do I have to do to get this notebook taken away? Just tell me.

The Lost Girls

MY SON WAKES ME UP, MOUTH CLOSE TO MY EAR.

"Our neighbor—" he hisses.

I jump in the dark.

"Our neighbor is really Amelia Earhart."

I flick the light. My boy is illuminated, encyclopedia in hand. White leather. Gold leaf letter.

Usually this is for some clue regarding the whereabouts of his mother.

He doesn't believe she's dead. The therapist says it's because he didn't see it happen.

I drew him a cartoon once of what happened and he said, "That's just a cartoon. Fake."

The frame with his mother on the gurney being loaded into the ambulance is especially fake. An ambulance never came. Just the coroner. But try explaining that to a little boy.

This time, and for the first time, he's not asking about Emily.

"Amelia Earhart, maybe," I say.

"It's definitely her! The first woman to fly around the world! We're going over there."

"No we are not. I've got work, you got school."

"You don't work, you draw."

"Isn't that a beautiful thing you just said."

He looks out the window. "Amelia Earhart's lights are on."

"So?"

"So! She just walked in front of the window!"

"Bed," I say and he leaves the room.

There's a noise outside, I crane my neck to the window. It's Walter knocking on the neighbor's door. When the door opens there is golden light and a figure. My son steps inside the house. I can't even yell. The door closes.

I'm barefoot in the street and there's glass and a dog, loose from some yard, roaming in the darkness, barking on the other side of the drainage pond.

I knock. The woman lets me in, her face wrapped in bandages. She says, "I just met your son ... He said he was researching a school project."

"On what?"

"Disappeared women. Missing women."

I glance around the room. Model airplanes suspended from fishing string. Bookcases. Painting of a beach covered in massive crabs, pinchers up.

"He's fine." She smiles behind the bandages. "I don't think I've ever even seen you."

"I don't go outside."

She shrugs this off. "I like your boy. I see him playing out in the yard. He asked me if I was Amelia Earhart. I told him I was. I hope that's okay. He's looking for evidence to show you."

I call Walter. I hear him call back, distantly.

The woman forces me to sit down on her couch.

We sit in stony silence while I look at her bandages.

"Plastic surgery," she says. I realize I've never gotten her real name and she hasn't got mine. I'm happy not knowing her true identity if I don't have to give up mine.

She slaps my leg, "I'm told I'll be even more unrecognizable."

"That's good," I say.

I hear the patter of feet on the stairs as Walter bounds down,

"Dad look what I found ..."

A book flops onto my lap.

The Collected Works of Linus Duncan: Ten Years of Ily and Lee.

"Your book."

Amelia Earhart is astounded. Here I am, the famous cartoonist who doesn't do famous anymore.

I say, "Well it's an equal privilege to finally meet the pilot of the Enola Gay."

"You're thinking of someone else," she says. "I haven't seen your comics in the paper any more. You still draw?"

"I do."

She says, "The comics in the paper are not good anymore. That makes me feel like world is not good anymore."

"The world is how we remember it," I say.

Walter taps the woman on the shoulder and says, "Why do you have so many books on airplanes?"

"Because I'm a pilot," she says. "My plane is at the airfield."

"You're a pilot for real?"

"I am," she says, "I can show you my pilot's license if you want to see. I've got a fake name now. But I promise you I'm the real thing."

She walks off. I should be telling my son he's rude and should leave the woman alone with his game, but the problem is, I'm weeping about a cartoon of my wife and I pushing a baby carriage on the beach, only the baby has hopped out of the carriage and is behind us in the surf about to be hit by a wave, swept away forever, and there is a sea lion in the carriage tossing a football up for itself to catch. I hide my face behind the book.

Before we leave, I have to sign in blood that we'll go for a flight in this imaginary plane with this imaginary woman.

And we do go flying on Wednesday.

Her plane dives out of the sky and lands in the middle of our quiet street. The propeller shreds the low lying limbs of the weeping willow, but no one minds that, we'd rather not weep.

My son charges down the hallway into my office where I am drawing. I have a new deadline I refuse to miss.

"I'm not going flying ..." but my son grabs my shirt and yanks me through the doorway, and once you're past the threshold, forget the threshold.

We climb inside her plane.

Her bandages are off and her face is smooth as the sea is at dawn.

Amelia puts the throttle down. Gaining speed until air is under the wings and suddenly we are high above our little assumed lives.

"Where would you like to go?" she asks us.

Walter says, "Where was she last seen?"

"No one knows."

So we just soar along. Just the sounds of the engines and the propellers.

Below us, in a field next to the supermarket, there is a little girl in a blue dress walking across the broken asphalt road. The field is lousy with wild flowers. Pink and yellow and white dots.

"What's she doing?"

"Trying to catch butterflies in her hands."

I press my face to the glass and say to everyone, "Yup. There she is."

"There who is?"

"Whoever you want it to be."

JANT

I WATCHED A WOMAN FIX A ROADSIDE SHRINE JUST before the rain came.

Blue and purple plastic flowers thinned by summer sun and bent weird by winter. Coat hangers built into a cross. Nailed into a swamp oak. Ya know.

We was parked in my car on the overpass and just watching.

Nothing to do. Flicking the air freshener of the nude firefighter. Me and Cindy do that sometimes. Park there. She tells me anecdotes. I flick the firefighter's balls.

You can see the most desperate parts of this town from up there.

Like the town's ribs poking out. Like the town's lazy eye. Like the town's bald spot. Can see the cars collide.

Cindy is a French inhaler, smoking her cigarette slow, exhale out the mouth and suck back in the nose. Pretend to be the cancerous tide to all in a wide arc from this perch, baby. And as she rests, following a laugh, and starts to tell me about one of her many many customers, I'm forced to lean over and shush her.

"What? What you ogre?"

"Look at this, the mother, I'm assuming the mother, look at her, very motherly, she's painting a message on the tree. A warning."

We watch, enthralled as each letter is formed with a big picket fence fan size brush, and Tom Sawyer whitewash, and the message says:

HER NAME
WAS JANT!
S P E E D
K I L L S !

"She spelled her own daughter's name wrong."

"Think she was hit by a car or you think she overdosed on yellow jackets?"

"Bees?"

"Speed," I say. "Meth."

"Oh."

"Car crashed through the shrine the other day. Heard it on the police scanner. Amazing how many wrecks happen here. This is like the car crash center of the universe."

"What a special thing to say about our town."

The woman packs her paints away in her station wagon because the rain has started and it is such an odd time to paint, right? There go the letters running down the tree, white streaks. As the car leaves I see it has decals in the window with the daughter's birthday year through her death year. She was just seventeen. Her name was spelled right on the back window.

Orange letters.

Red tail lights.

Blobs of water from green clouds.

I pop a ginger ale and pour it in both our coffee mugs. Her's says "I'm A Winner," mine is plain pink. Cindy dumps in some bourbon. She even has a bag of popcorn. We can't afford the movies but at this part of the curve there's often a free show.

"I feel bad," she says, "how excited I get about seeing something horrible happen. Does that make me a lousy person?"

"Nope." I take a drink from the cup and swish the ginger ale and liquor around violently in my mouth so I can feel the sharp pains in my teeth where the holes are. It's like hide and go seek.

"Hey, what's the nicest thing you ever did for anybody?"

"Nicest, oh I told you."

"Tell again."

"Well remember when I said I was a night guard on Parkerstown Bridge when I was studying to do the nurse thing that fell through?"

I nod. "I do. I do."

"This one night, there was this guy who stopped his car and he walked out to the sidewalk, and climbed over the little railing, and I yelled for him just before I guess he was gonna jump. But he didn't jump because of some bullshit I said. You remember this story?"

"Partly. Did you tell him there was sharks in the river?"

"No, I said he would survive the fall. I said he'd most likely just break his legs or pelvis and wouldn't drown. That he'd just be hurt. Hurt so bad. Make his situation worse."

"So he didn't jump."

"He did not. All because I told him, well more like sold him on the idea of a better death bridge I'd gone over with Walter when he was still alive. Costa Rica and there was crocodiles or alligators at the bottom of the bridge and it was a high fall and me and Walter threw chicken pieces off the bridge and the crocs went crazy. The jumper seemed real impressed by this far off bridge."

"That was real sweet. So the guy went to Costa Rica and killed himself?"

"Nah, I see him around sometime. But he put on some weight."

"We all do."

I look over at Cindy and she looks completely neutral. She is the most neutral life form on earth. She is not coming or going. She is not building up or tearing apart. The smoke comes out of her lips and circles back through her nose, in and out, an infinity symbol with no eye makeup or college degree.

Me, I'm mostly a division symbol.

I flick the firefighter right in his face. Anybody who calls themselves a hero, or believes they are one, is lost.

Pentagram

SAM DOESN'T BELIEVE.

She's so against Christmas she wants to torch a toy store, reduce it to ash, or whatever plastic becomes when it melts.

"People already bought their junk," I say. "Maybe next year. Plan early."

"Steal me a calendar."

We're sitting on the frozen concrete, our backs against a brick wall behind DrugVille.

We don't have prescriptions, but we have a desire for all of them.

The temperature is falling. It's not too bad. The wind's blocked by a dumpster.

My ass is asleep. My childhood friends are all dead, probably. Rudolph the Red-Nosed Reindeer was a woman.

Real people die climbing up or down chimneys. Mostly burglars and jealous lovers. Mechanical asphyxiation. Their lungs can't expand because they're not magic elf lungs.

What happens is you're led down corridors into a maze of baffling turns that drag you away from the you who sat on your daddy's shoulders to get a closer look at the North Star.

Sam is from here. She didn't have to leave home to fall flat on her glowing face.

"Let's go to the mall and bleed on people," she says.

"Not in the mood."

Feathers fall out of her puffy coat where she was stabbed. The wound is all healed, but the feathers keep coming out.

It's Christmas Eve. I don't want to bleed on anyone but I want to make Sam happy, and not just because I need her to keep me warm in the cardboard dumpster later.

For my birthday, she gave me a cat. He lived with us in Tent City, under the power lines.

When the cops raided Tent City, the cat ran into the woods.

Haven't seen him since. Smart cat. Renegade cat. Power broker cat.

Cops caught the rest of us.

When I'm as high as I wanna be, I picture that cat finding himself a better life. A nice office job. A little herringbone suit. Convertible cat car. T-tops, maybe. He drives around blasting The Beach Boys. Hot cat wife and a beautiful litter in a house—a fucking house!

Here we are, so damn stupid we can't help ourselves enough to walk west, find warmth on our filthy bodies.

Sam has an anarchy symbol tattooed on her left tit. She has an inverted cross on her right tit. It terminates at her inverted nipple.

"Lets jack decorations off people's lawns," Sam says. "Pawn that shit."

My jaw hurts. My left hand hurts. My knee, recently dislocated, swells.

"I'm not moving." I pet her green hair. "Give me your lighter."

She thinks I have something to smoke. I don't.

I light our propane torch and put it between us so we're warmer, and I ask, "How's that?"

"I'm in love," she says.

I keep my Christmas present for her in my pocket.

A brass pentagram welded onto the tip of a screwdriver. The guy at the hardware shop made it for me in exchange for shoveling his walk.

The bells have stopped. There'd been a woman shaking bells all afternoon. She'd been asking for money, but now she's gone. At least she wasn't holiday music.

There's always someone somewhere screaming, just on the edge of earshot. You can choose to listen or you can ignore it.

When Sam isn't looking I heat the pentagram in the propane flame until it turns white hot.

Sam nods off, twitching, caught in an edge of the tundra, the hopeless, icy igloo of a dream.

"Give me your hand," I say.

She opens her eyes, smiles when she sees the glowing pentagram.

"Oh, fucking-A, babe."

Part of me hopes it will snow. Another part hopes it won't.

Sam pulls off her glove and exposes her milky wrist.

Her veins are flat, almost invisible. But I can see every tooth in her mouth.

The hiss of singeing flesh whispering, "Hail Satan."

She hugs me for a while.

The pentagram throbs pink. I press an empty bottle against her skin to cool it.

She says, "You're so nice to me and I can't understand why."

I say, "I can't figure out why you're nice to me, either."

"For revenge."

"Revenge. Always. Big revenge."

Sam leans into me. Also, she's getting a rock out from under her butt. She flings it at the dumpster.

"Know what I want to give you, babe?" she says. "I wanna give you a world eradicated by nuclear war." She wipes the snot from her nose. "Clean slate."

The bells start up again. Distant. Constant.

"Imagine how nice it'd be if the whole world just died in a wild flash?" Sam says. "And it was just me and you, sitting here with nothing. Then we'd be standing up and peeking around the brick wall, looking down the street and seeing no traffic lights or cops, jobs, seagulls, bells, taxes, or any other people for forever. Wouldn't it be nice?"

The Paralyzer

THE NIGHT THEY TOOK HIS FATHER OFF LIFE support, we scaled the fence and went to the top of the Paralyzer. Not trying to die. But something blurry and near that.

The water was off in the park, but we did the hundred and seventy-five foot drop down the tallest slide, on burlap sacks, screaming and eyes clenched and oh my god oh my god.

I'd stolen the burlap sacks from the hardware store I worked at. They had Italia stamped on them because they'd come from Italy. *Cazzuto.*

Get this, they used the burlap sacks to stuff between valuable fountains and statues that were shipped in wooden boxes bigger than me and this was the funny part, people, most of them Italians anyway, bought the statues to stick in front of their beachfront summer homes, either placing them at the base of the driveway or on the back of the house facing the ocean.

My whole plan in life had been to replace Scott on the forklift at the hardware store when he went to college, but he never went and neither did I. He's probably still driving that forklift, good for him, the privileged little shit.

I lost that job because I sometimes sledgehammered those statues apart for fun after work to feel better about myself.

Here's some hard science—did you know, the terrifying ride down The Paralyzer was at least three times faster than when the water was on and the park was stuffed with city kids come down to Jersey for the weekend? On a burlap sack, water off, you could go down the slide like a greased blur. Without the resistance of the fat chlorinated water, your ass got hot and your hair blew back and your face got all taut and you forgot how your mom was fucking the garbage man and your dad had gone off to another nightly news war zone. The drop on a regular day felt like one thousand feet. Now the drop felt like a million feet.

Hollllllllllly shiiiiiiiiiit!

When we got to the bottom, the trough that usually slowed everyone down was empty of water and we went sailing onto the concrete.

Bouncing. Skidding. Elbows and knees skinned.

Blood cascading off ripped flesh.

But Mike jumped up, and said, "Let's do that again!"

Up the cling clang structure we sprinted.

So strange, all my memories being resurrected by the local paper.

Yesterday I read about the park in the paper, the slide burnt to the ground, and it surprised me to see it was only a hundred and five foot drop from the ground level to the top of the highest water slide in Splash Castle.

But the night Mike and I had the park to ourselves was the night his father lost his battle to an unidentifiable malady. There was a heat lightning storm, too—the sky over Seaside Heights, the weirdest purple. Green clouds over the Sky Lift. Pink lightning looked like it was kissing the tip of Arcade Pier.

Climb a hundred and seventy steps(?) and at the top, we could reach out and pluck down the emerald clouds like cotton candy.

From the top of the structure, we could see the boardwalk, and the ocean smashing against the sand. We could see the Ferris wheel and the Human Slingshot that flung people out over the ocean in a basket and then pulled them back to safety with great rubber bands. I could see all the stands where I'd lost my newspaper delivery money trying to win a Game Boy or a Walkman or even a stuffed heart to give to any of the girls in my class who didn't know what my house looked like.

And from the top of the Paralyzer I could see Mike's equally shitty house just three blocks away. A doomed bungalow with trash in the yard blown by a bay breeze that never stopped long enough to warrant picking up the trash. The lights were off because his mom was at the hospital.

Another thing I just read in the newspaper yesterday—his mom remarried twice after that. Both times, the husbands wound up in critical care. She was putting poison in their Gatorades. Or in the case of the third husband, in his nightly scotch and water. Eventually everything you do taps you on the shoulder and you have to turn around and face it.

Thing is, you never really know anything, or anybody for that matter, until they save you, or try to kill you.

The Paralyzer had two fiberglass tracks. When the water in the park was on, it was fun to stand at the bottom and watch the people (who thought they were the bravest!) race each other down. It was also fun to watch the girls who would come down with their suits ripping off or their suits giving them wedgies. I was missing a front tooth back then, this was the best I could do.

But that night, the park was deserted and it was just Mike and I and he was always getting into trouble and this time he had me along to get in trouble with him and I didn't mind because I was bored too. All the statues smashed. All the banana peels smoked, to no effect. Five dollars worth of quarters stolen out of parked cars along Sherman Avenue, windows left open, New York plates. Go fuck yourself. We couldn't afford the Human Slingshot, so here we were.

This was our fourth time down the slide, and over the fence, out on the main drag, we could see the cop cars that had shown up with their lights not even flashing. The cops were standing on the sidewalk looking up at us on the top of the structure. I wondered which of the neighbors on the drag had seen us. I scanned the street, saw a woman and a man standing in their yard smoking cigarettes, looking up too. I'd key their yellow Camaro the next day.

"We have to go down to run," Mike said.

"Okay! 1-2-3..."

We launched down the twin slides of The Paralyzer and when we hit the ground, I ripped my leg all up on the concrete.

The cops still couldn't get in the gate, and even better for us, we knew how to get out of the park without having to go back over the fence.

If you go into the maintenance room hidden behind Black Burt's Cave, you can squeeze past the PVC plumbing pipes and the giant pool filters that pump water to Lazy Lagoon, and if you're wild enough, you can pull up the grating and you can crawl through a small tunnel that goes out underneath the sidewalk and across the street and into the storm drain in the dirt parking lot that charges you $5 for the whole day, rather than fighting the meter.

You just walk in the sewer for half a block pretending like you're a Ninja Turtle; there's even a ladder and a sewer lid on Mike's street. His dog did look like a giant rat that could teach you things if you got high enough and listened.

Up on the street, we ducked behind cars and watched the cops as they waited for the manager to come with the key.

This was a good distraction on the night Mike's dad left the earth. Getting away, this is one of my only triumphant memories.

Last winter I saw Mike at the county mall. It's been going on twenty years. Strange how radically people can mutate when you don't think about them.

I'm a little embarrassed to admit that I was working part time at the mall that Christmas, doing gift wrapping outside of Sears. It's not like I'm a great gift wrapper or anything, but they were only paying $8 an hour, so I don't think they were expecting the best anyway. No one cared that I was gin blossomed and listening to a Public Enemy cassette tape with my headphones on.

Mike walked up with a board game, Mouse Trap. I didn't even know they still made Mouse Trap.

He recognized me, I didn't recognize him at first. I took my headphones off. His voice had changed octaves.

Mike wasn't the mile a minute kid I remembered from middle school with a fade haircut and a lightning bolt on the side of his head. His face was doughy and wounded.

He had his hair combed in a part. He wore a pink satin suit.

The woman he held hands with was five inches taller than him. He introduced her as Lilly and later, at his chiropractic office, he confided in me that she was 'the greatest Vietnamese lover I've ever had.'

He'd grown a mustache and looked like a pedo. But I guess he could look at me and say, "What happened to the rest of his teeth?" and, "Is that a pint in your pocket or are you happy to see me?"

Before he left the mall he handed me a card for his chiropractic services and I said, "I'm fine, really, my back is great. Have never had a problem."

He looked at me all funny and he said, "It's not just for your back, you know."

He thought that chiropractic medicine could cure any disease, which is just about the most insane thing I'd ever heard in my life.

I don't know why I thought that way because I'd been to acupuncture three times. There used to be a little storefront in the strip mall by the tire shop.

Each time I went for acupuncture, it was different.

I had terrible acne all the way up to when I started sandblasting at Millville Machinist. They put the needles in my palms. Hundreds of needles. And in a month my skin was clear, but it might have been from the sandblasting too. I'd been fired by the time the month was over. I don't know.

I tried to quit drinking once. They put the needles, five needles in each ear. That worked for a day, but then the drinking got worse.

Another time, over a long winter, when my fiancé was on the verge of leaving me, even circling an 'end date' on a calendar she brought over to my room at The Shamrock Motel … I couldn't get an erection. In desperation I went again to the acupuncturist and the guy put a needle behind my left knee, another right over my heart, a final one into my throat, the Adam's apple. That worked for the thing with my dick, but my fiancé still left. Took the calendar with her.

Who knows what magic is?

After Christmas, when all the gift wrapping was done and I needed rent, I got a different job, working overnights at the aerosol spray can factory in the industrial park. The shift manager who hired me gave me a photocopied piece of paper with three different clinics I could go to to get a drug test.

I was clean at the time but still nervous to take a test. I've failed every test of my little life. So when I recognized one of the testing places as Mike's chiropractic office, I went there without thinking twice about it.

There was a beat up diesel BMW in the driveway. Gold. The house had two flags hung by the door, one with the Italian flag, the other with a lotus flower on a tie-dyed backdrop.

The chiropractic office was around the back though, and down a little set of brick steps slowly turning back into clay dust.

His office was in the basement of a lonely old house, junk stacked in all the windows I could see into. I assumed he was living upstairs. In one of the windows I could see that A Tribe Called Quest poster I remembered from his bedroom. The house had rose gardens, the flowers shriveled up and uncared for. A Buddha statue with the left arm snapped off. This house reminded me of his mother's house by Splash Castle, but stretched out like silly putty pulled to its maximum.

Maybe it was just the garden that reminded me of his mom's grimy bungalow, and how she'd kept a lot of plants. Mike had grown a marijuana plant there in the garden and it grew so tall and stuck out like a sore thumb but no one ever said anything because they either felt bad about his dead dad or they didn't know what a marijuana plant looked like.

Strange now, they're everywhere. You see kids walking around the boardwalk wearing t-shirts with marijuana leaves on them and you see kids driving around in cars with bumper stickers with pot plants all on them basically taunting the cops. I don't even look cross-eyed at a cop, let alone taunt one. I've always assumed I got lucky that one time by beating them, and I have no other luck left with them or anybody else.

Before I could even ring the doorbell, Mike flung the door open. He shook my hand and pulled me inside. He was wearing the pink suit still, but a lime green dress shirt underneath. We were in our late thirties that day but I almost laughed when I saw he still walked the same. In the halls of Central Regional High School people called him Monkey Mike because he walked like a chimpanzee or something—kind of slouched forward and arms dangling. Here he was, time spanned like a blink, still the same walk.

But the last time we'd hung out before that, we were kids, just seventeen, screwing around with cars that were driving down Double Trouble Road.

I've never told anyone this, but we caused a pretty severe wreck.

We had a fake flashing light on the top of the car that we got at a novelty shop in the mall and he was driving. I was in the passenger seat as he gassed it good, chasing a car for no reason, in the rain, sun falling behind the pines. I remember laughing, reaching across the car and pounding the steering wheel so the horn blasted out all sinister. At the bend, the car skidded off the asphalt and struck a tree head on. We kept driving.

At a table in Fried Paradise, we stared at dead pieces of chicken and crinkle fries covered in red goo. We listened to the real cop cars, the ambulances, the fire trucks as they blasted down route 9 towards the tragedy we'd caused and I'm only writing about this now to you because I love you and trust you and I'm plastered and hope you don't repeat it. Feel like I could have gone to jail five times for the stupid things we did when we were kids.

Last night, I lay in the dark and drank a six pack in bed, thinking about those people in that car. Who were they? Did they survive? I guess I could look it up at the library on the film machine, old newspapers. But I think I'd probably do something bad to myself if I saw what I think happened. I'd rather just pretend it was all a bad dream. Or that I'm in the dream now and if I wake up I'll get punished by some cosmic judgement more potent and bizarre than I can comprehend here.

It's as if each of these beer bottles contains a dose of magic that keeps reality hidden in the fuzzy shadow of water parks, and boardwalks, and the sweet confectioner sugar stink of zeppoles fried at the stand across from the carousel. For my thirtieth birthday, a woman I nearly married paid for me to go to the dentist and get an impression of my gums made, false teeth made from that. I have the false teeth somewhere, but I don't wear them. They hurt me. Everything in the present hurts me. Oh wait, I don't have the teeth ... I just remembered what I did with them. I smashed them with a baseball bat on my thirty-fifth birthday. Edge of the frozen boardwalk. Ferris wheel dark.

I don't think Mike was ever the same after that accident. We never talked about it, and never would for as long as he was alive.

And there in the basement chiropractic office all these years later, I could see it firsthand. How much he'd vanished and been replaced by a pod person with a blank mind, coping. Same walk though, ha. And he had no shoes on, was barefoot on a dirty rug that I could feel through my work boots, even.

There was a cramped waiting room, stuffed with hundreds of magazines, "Need anything to read? Take some of these with you when you go. Lilly gets them from the trash. She's an angel."

Something was different, something I hadn't noticed in the mall. He spoke slower. He spoke as if stuck in half-speed. Brow perpetually soaked with sweat.

The kid who I'd known was gone, but I wondered what he saw when he saw me.

We all go to sleep and wake up totally different. Strangers walking through the wreckage. Odd ducks tiptoeing beyond the debris. People with eyes closed in the $2 cinemas of our own random lives.

"How's your back?" he said.

"The back is good," I said. "No problems there."

I showed him the paperwork for the factory.

He looked at the paperwork for a long time.

"You can pass a drug test?"

"Yeah," I said.

He nodded, seemed impressed.

"I've got synthetic piss if you need it." I declined. "A factory? What will you do there?"

"Drive the forklift I hope ..."

"Didn't you do that when we were kids? Over at the hardware store?"

"Just once, I fucked up and a crate slipped off and crushed the back of this guy's pickup truck."

"Better luck this time."

He stared through me for a minute and I got uncomfortable.

I said, "Okay, give me the cup or whatever. I'll fill it and you'll finally get to see my piss up close. It'll be a whole new chapter for us."

He faked a laugh, got the cup.

I went into the bathroom and the light didn't work, but it didn't matter. There was daylight sneaking in from a window almost obscured by things piled up against it outside. After the piss test, a special cap screwed on the plastic jar, and a test strip showed I wasn't obliterated on ten different separate things, Mike said, "Come on, I'll show you my office."

His office was wood paneled and stunk like mold. The walls were covered in posters showing different traumas of the spine. Everywhere

I looked was a different skeleton. A different stack of cartoon vertebrae. A separate way the rungs of human life can be pulled randomly off a happy ladder to smash into/onto a hard surface. Pain waits in the wings to overtake wellbeing. Some people, they just never walk again.

Mike opened his drawer and took out a pipe. He started packing it with weed from a ziplock.

He lit the pipe with a match. Took a deep hit.

He passed the pipe to me. I had a clean bill of health and a job in the morning, so I went for it.

I smoked. Eyes narrowed. He reached behind him and pushed play on the stereo. A cassette whirred to life. Something exotic.

"That's nice," I said. "What are those instruments?" I pointed at the stereo as if the stereo was another person sitting in the room, someone to love and teach me things.

"Đàn b ̀âu, and Đàn đáy." The music on the tape sounded like the scars of the world being melted off by sunshine and waterfalls. Waves of glowing birds. In came the flutes.

"Dandy. Gotta get me one of those." I leaned back. "You still play guitar?"

He held up his hand. His middle finger and ring finger were gone on his left hand.

"Did you know that the passage of time is like a demolition derby? No one wins."

"No one wins a demolition derby?" I said, surprised, I never thought about it. "I think someone has to win it, or why do it?"

He shrugged. His jaw was slack. His tongue like a slide.

The weed was mixed with PCP, but he hadn't told me that. We sat there for probably two hours, talking, blabbing, drooling, but I can't remember a single thought or a single word. It was a visit that unvisited itself. When Lilly's footsteps were heard upstairs, our little pow wow next to the maps of the spine was over. He slapped his palm across the tape deck and the paradise popped off. "This was fun," he said.

On my way up the brick steps, back to the street, I tripped over my own feet and went face first into the rose bushes. Cut my moneymaker all up. But no one saw. And no one asked what happened.

It was the one time in my life I've taken a cab, left my car parked there on the street. Chalk that up to fear and personal growth. The cabbie was parked a block away in the lot of Food Universe. I begged him to take me home. He was in the middle of a sandwich. I climbed in the back of the car, and waited until he was finished with his sandwich.

When he was finished, he threw the trash out the window. Seagulls descended in a swarm.

"Where we going?"

"Double Trouble Road," I said. "Drive me into a tree, fast as you can."

"Get the fuck out of my car."

"Shamrock Motel then," I said.

"Seven dollars. And show me it now."

I held the money up. He reached back and grabbed it.

"Not another word, fruit loop."

There is security footage of The Paralyzer being burnt to the ground. The news keeps showing it, like someone will sing.

In the video, a man in a pink suit appears on the concrete walking underneath the purple and yellow slides that wrap together in the sky like twisty straws.

I am surprised that I don't know what the twisty straws were called. Now it's too late. They're just called Melted Molten Goop. They're called ash in a dumpster.

The man in the pink suit is carrying a jug of fuel in his left hand. As he starts to climb the structure you can see him in the footage as he gets to the first platform and switches hands, carrying the jug of fuel in his right all the way to the very top.

At the top of the structure, he takes something out of his back pocket and no one is sure exactly what it is. The police don't have any idea, but I know it is a burlap sack from Sal's hardware just around the corner.

At the top of the structure, the figure begins to dump the jug of fuel all the way down the slide.

He lights a match, the slide goes up in a whoosh of fire.

The figure plummets down on the burlap sack and goes screaming through the flames all the way to the bottom of the Paralyzer.

He does a tumble onto the concrete, pops up, pats himself off—and in the footage, is seen sprinting back up the structure one last time.

Rye

MY GIRL, TRACEY, HAS THREE KIDS, BUT NONE OF them are hers. She found these kids. It's none of my business, really. It's none of your business, either. Hey, I'm sorry I even mentioned it.

She alleges to have found the first boy, Evel, down in the drainage ditch behind her parents' house. She was suntanning on the roof of their house, and from that high point she saw baby Evel below, moving through a very low gully. He was crawling in the reeds like an animal in hunt.

Tracey's parents were at Disneyland. They've gone there every year since Tracey's dad turned 40. They never took Tracey there as a child.

I don't think you really can prove your love to anybody. It's my opinion that each of us has a personal responsibilities to find a near miraculous satisfaction in every foul and ugly thing, passing itself off as man, beast, or whatever other cursed object; otherwise, being alive, in summary, probably just means being destroyed every time you dare to blink.

So, I'm supposed to feel bad about all this Disneyland blather, but I just don't.

I tell Tracey, "The place is horrible, babe. I've been there twice."

I've also told her I've been to Afghanistan, two missions, but can say no more. I'll admit it to you though, I couldn't even find Afghanistan on a map. Sometimes you just say things. Sometimes you just eat an American flag for breakfast, and one for lunch, and another for dinner.

Drainage ditch, back to the drainage ditch.

There was Evel, naked and covered in green mud, just slopping around on his belly. Tracey walked out into the high grass of the yard, and carefully made her way down the embankment in her neon bikini, and she bent down and pulled Evel right out of the muck, so his body made a kind of sucking sound—and that's how Tracey first became a mother.

That boy is good at drawing and loves to dance around the house. He's not hypnotized by the Nintendo like his 'brother' Jim, and doesn't sunlight bounce or moonlight trampoline like 'sister' Kim. Seven years old, Evel still hunts around the outside of the trailer on his belly like he's stalking some invisible force. Some things you never outgrow.

We found baby Jim, and baby Kim lying shirtless on their backs in the red hot Food Universe lot. Tracey was going to pull into a parking spot. We almost ran the babies over. But I screamed, "Stop!" And Evel saw too, he screamed, "Babies! Stop!"

As a family unit, we carried the sweaty babies into the store and even stood in line at the customer service desk, holding the thrashing newborns. Music played over the speaker system of the store, and someone at the desk was pleading for a raincheck. I never once recall a true belief that we were capable of shucking our duty to the helpless and passing it off back into the abyss that constitutes the wide web of this hurtful world. So when the lady at the help desk said, "Can I help you?" I said, "No! Never mind." We left the store, and Evel didn't even get the Slip 'N Slide that was his reward for a good first report card in school.

Tracey drove. I held these two babies. Kim all cross-eyed at first, and Jim with his lone tooth. But they were docile babies. And they were lovely babies. And Evel even cradled Kim in his room that night and I explained to him, "Probably you shouldn't mention these babies at school."

"Why?"

"People might get angry."

"Cause we're lucky to find such nice babies?"

"That, yeah, a little that."

"What else?"

"We should have called the cops."

"Why?"

"It's just what you're supposed to do."

"Why?" he said.

"Why what?" I said.

"Why what why?"

"You're getting it. You understand existence." I patted his sweaty head. "You do."

And Evel pinched my arm where my rose tattoo is. For a long time he was testing me, trying to cause me pain. Back then, I was posing as an Army Ranger, not a clerk at the Dollar Store. Army Rangers feel no pain.

In the other room I heard Tracey with Jim bouncing on her knee and she said, "You're a good baby, yes you are. I'm going to take you somewhere nice soon," she hissed this, like the snake swinging down out of the Tree of Life, "Disssssneyland."

Enoch

THE DOG BARKS ALL NIGHT. THE DOG STILL BARKS at dawn, noise echoing off blue mountains. They step into the gray light, stare across the valley from the stone porch.

"Those people must be jerkoffs," the girl says. Dan looks down at his sister, wonders where she picked that up.

"Don't say that."

"Why?" Allie says.

"Doesn't mean what you think it means."

"Means they should let their dog in because it's cold."

And look at her go, walking down the gravel driveway. She has on her purple ballerina shoes, glitter'd. He sits down on the swing, crosses his arms so as not to shiver. He doesn't want to chop the firewood yet. After breakfast.

They are supposed to decide which of them is going to go and live with dad, in the desert, in binocular view of palm trees in the distance, where there is no snow and where there is no mom.

And which of them is going to stay here, where there is no dad, and the piano is untuned, but the three of them sometimes sing songs from The Muppets, also out of tune.

The dog begins to lose its voice. And the snow out the window is not white, it is blue.

"I'm gonna set her free!" Allie sings, charging out the door.

"Don't!"

"Free!"

She gets smaller and smaller. Now just a figurine in the distance, running the rest of the way down the gravel road. He takes out a rolled cigarette from dad's abandoned army coat and is discouraged by life when he realizes it's just a cigarette and not a joint.

Allie opens the front gate and walks up the steps. Last year's Christmas wreath, brown needles. The dog barks even more viciously, tearing at the backyard chainlink. No one answers the door.

Dan watches his sister leap off the steps like a skier doing a long jump. Watches her trot towards the driveway again. But at the last second, she pivots, she opens the gate.

The dog sprints out, runs circles around her as she laughs.

Her name is Enoch. Female. The breed is indecipherable, but she reminds the kids of those dogs that King Tut had. She eats the pillows on the couch. She knocks the aquarium over, but the fish have all died long ago, water drained. Allie screams at Enoch running through the broken glass but no one gets hurt. Enoch can even run over broken glass it seems. They know her name because she has a tattoo on her belly. Enoch. A real rough job too.

Dan says, "You shouldn't have stolen this dog."

"No one cares about her."

"They cared enough to tattoo her."

"That means they don't care."

"Lots of ways of looking at it."

Dan tosses logs into the fire place and Enoch tries to catch the sparks as they float, eyes manic, jaws snapping.

Allie yells from mom's room, "Found out why they call her that. Religious freaks! It's from the Bible!"

"What?"

"Book of Enoch. Cain's son. Or an angel, I don't know."

"How do you know?"

"Google."

"Get off the computer."

There's silence for a minute.

Allie yells, "Gross! Hahaha, you were right about 'jerk off'!"

"GET OFF THE COMPUTER!"

Dan plays his guitar in his room all day. Allie dances on the couch, bounds throughout the living room, sprints up and down the hallway. The dog chases.

It's how she used to play with Sarah when Dad lived there with Sarah too.

For a minute, while Allie is in the bathroom, Enoch claws at Dan's door while he strums the guitar. He can't decide if he wants to let the dog in. When the dog starts to howl along with the guitar, Dan opens the door by stretching his foot and rotating the door knob with an outstretched socked toe.

Mom comes home at 3 o'clock in the morning. Enoch runs out of the shadows and gives her a heart attack. She slams on the floor. She jumps on her. She licks her glasses off. She smells her hair. Mom screams. The children leap out of bed.

"Dad gave us the dog!"

"Yes! Dad gave us the dog!"

"Calm down!"

"USPS special delivery! We swear!"

"Calm down!"

"My birthday present!"

"Put down the hot poker!"

"Stop!"

Mom plops in a chair in the dining room, pops the wine bottle. Smiles in defeat. Enoch sleeps at her feet.

The red pickup truck is in the driveway down the valley. A man in a white baseball cap is on his front porch, whistling.

Allie pets Enoch's head.

She says, "Don't worry, you're my friend now."

She doesn't say what.

The man whistles again. The dog puts her head down on Allie's purple shoe.

The next day Dan sees a flyer for the lost dog at the music store. There's another one at his elementary school. Allie cries when she sees the flyer stapled to the telephone pole at her bus stop.

"Why are you crying?" Lisa asks.

"I'm not," she says, ripping the flyer down, stuffing it into her lunch box.

It snows like the end of the world. Mom calls and the factory is loud behind her. "I'm sleeping here," she says. "You'll be okay till morning?"

"Got the firewood in before it started."

"And you have the soup in the fridge. Make your sister eat a handful of broccoli. I don't care if you have to threaten to cut her hair off while she sleeps. Just make her eat it."

"Okay."

Allie is on the floor, drawing in a notebook.

"What are you making?"

"Blueprints for Enoch."

"What's that mean?"

"One of those obstacle courses. Fire for her to jump through. A slide to slide down. A pool that she can jump into, soaring, catch a frisbee."

"That won't work, Allie," Dan says.

"Of course it will."

"The neighbor will see his dog and come back for him. The guy in the white hat. The whistler."

"I'm not stupid," she says. "I'll have to build this at daddy's. I'll have to go there and live. Only way."

She keeps drawing.

"You'll have to share a room with Sarah again."

"I don't care."

"Maybe I do."

Dan pours equal amounts of soup into the bowls, bumps the microwave open with his sharp elbow.

They lie on the couch, trying to stay warm by the fire. The TV won't work now. A board game is on the floor. Sorry. Pieces missing. They might play, they might not. First they'd have to search the house for alternative things to use as pieces: mom's lipstick, dad's forgotten cufflinks kept on mom's dresser, dryer lint rolled into a ball, kept together with a rubber band; the spire from the castle out of the smashed aquarium.

"I don't think you'd be happy living with dad," Dan says.

"I'm going to make a saddle for Enoch and ride through the base, chasing unlucky little desert animals."

That was the other thing, dad lived on a military base.

"Do you think they'll make me go to war?" she says.

"You're already in it."

The boy looked across the room at the piano and wondered how many fire crackers it would take to make the entire thing burst apart in one final flash.

There's a knock on the door.

The dog starts to bark. They both jump. She hasn't barked in days.

The door is not locked.

The door opens.

"Hello?"

It's the man in the white baseball cap. His face is angry.

He is coming into the house.

There're his shoes and there's his body.

The dog's teeth are flashing in a whirlwind. Enoch attacks the man. He yells out in surprise.

They spill out onto the porch, propelled out of the house, into the ice storm.

His head strikes the bottom step.

His body is suddenly limp.

The dog sniffs the still body.

The children watch at the window. They let the dog back in. Brush the snow off her. They think about what to do. But after a little while, the man begins to move again, he groans and rubs his head. Enoch whines at the window. They open the door to let the dog back out. The man and his dog leave together, walking back to the house down the hill.

And not too soon after that, the children are split from each other, too.

Scanner

LAST NIGHT, JUST AS A CALL CAME IN ON THE scanner, I was thirty feet tall, and I had a mouth full of red light. It was 4am. Like it always is.

The dispatcher said, "Domestic dispute, 601 Division Street. Any units available?"

No response.

I stopped mopping to glance at the cartoon street map that hung on the wall. Division Street is right behind the facility.

One time I posed as a garbage man, rode along with the other garbage men. They didn't care. They let me pick up the heavy cans. High-fived me with wet hands.

I took home a smashed TV. Still watch it in my cramped room.

Another time I got an orange vest, a yellow hard hat, spiky shoes, and scaled a telephone pole outside my ex-girlfriend's house. Climbed right up to the buzzing electric lines. Waited and watched her glowing house.

I could see shadows walking past the window, and isn't that your whole life? Being a shadow walking past a window?

Love is not a riddle you solve with another riddle.

I leaned out and kissed the step-down transformer box.

I licked the transformer. Bit onto the black wires. Buzzing. Humming. Reached up and grabbed higher wires with my hands, hanging like a heartbroken ape.

Guess I can't die.

"Anyone?" the dispatcher on the police scanner said, desperate, "Domestic Dispute, 601 Division ..."

I'm not a cop, but I go.

I visualize two squad cars parked in 69 behind Food Universe. Four napping cops. Drooling on themselves.

It's the time of morning when society changes its bandages.

I javelin the mop into the hallway and take off my shirt, change into my cop costume. Shirt, hat, badge, baton, replica rubber gun. Taser.

The boiler room is vibrating on auto pilot. I'll just be twenty minutes. This'll be fun.

I slip out the back and sprint between the medical waste dumpster and the chainlink fence and then I'm on the street.

Pumping my arms like I'm splitting molecules.

The house is just a couple blocks up. I count down from 1000 with the mailboxes.

The woman is on the front steps, sitting quietly, recently she was weeping. I can smell it. Taste it in the air. Braided black hair and a canary yellow bridesmaid dress (my guess).

She stands when she sees me walking up the driveway. She is barefoot.

"Problem?" I ask, careful not to huff and puff.

"I need to get in my house," she says. "He won't let me in my house."

"Who?"

"Darryl."

There're headlights coming up the block and for a minute I get nervous it's a squad car but it isn't. It's the milkman.

I wave.

The milkman doesn't wave back.

"Does anyone have a weapon here?" I ask the woman.

"What? No. Just you."

"Perfect. What do you need out of the house?"

"Some clothes. Some personal items."

I shine my flashlight and get a proper look and notice that the woman's bottom lip is fat from being hit. There is dried blood in her nostrils.

"Personal items? That mean drugs?"

She looks away.

"I don't care, I'll get your drugs, your clothes, photo albums. Whatever you want."

The window opens upstairs. A man leans out, shirtless. "I've got a restraining order against her."

"His own wife!"

"Allison, shut your mouth."

I hold my hand to my lips, sssssh. "Sir, come down here and open the door, or I'll blow your house up with nitroglycerin, metaphorically."

"What?"

I take the gun off my hip. I wave it up at him.

The man, like most people, is hypnotized by the gun, or not this gun because it is rubber, but the thought of a gun. He comes down and unlocks the door. Apologizes. Says his father is a cop.

I say, "Well, I'm not your daddy."

We're inside now. Me and Allison. Walking room to room with a purple backpack. She points, I put things in the bag.

I've told the shirtless man to pour himself a drink in the kitchen and to stay in there.

"We'll just be a hot minute."

Being inside someone's home when they don't want you there fills me with birdsong, explosion fireworks, skeletal bliss.

"He cheated on me."

"I have experience with that," I say, taking her hand. "Girl I knew became a mechanized shadow. Her face once beautiful to me turned to snow static like a TV station gone off air. Where she stepped, green ooze bubbled up. It's like that with you and your guy?"

Allison stares at me. "Something like that."

"I'm not just a cop. I'm also a therapist."

"Cool."

"It gets easier," I say. "Try drawing a picture of him being carried away by wasps or vultures."

"I will. I'll try that."

But now she is looking closer at my badge. Closer at my face. Her eyes dart from spot to spot. She'd make a lousy magician. Or poker player. Or believer of any kind.

Dishes ricochet in the sink in the near distance. I hear Darryl yelling.

We end up in their bedroom.

She opens the top drawer and takes all the condoms out, puts them in the bag. I reach on the night stand and take the remote control to Darryl's TV and throw it out the window.

"He hit you? You want me to hit him?"

"No," she says. "I hit him too. I kicked him in the balls and then he knocked me over and yanked my boots off, threw them in the garden."

"Fair enough."

He's quiet and standing there and suddenly she doesn't live there anymore, so I think I see a smile, but it's hard to tell because her swollen lip is trembling.

"Thank you," she says, but I realize that means she is done, the backpack is full and it is time to leave. I get sad. But then the fear returns because I know reality has flipped the light switch back on again—such heavy shame.

I hear the faint squeak of brakes. Out the window I see a real cop coming.

"Allison," I say, "Go in the bathroom and lock the door. It's for your own safety. I think he has a gun." She listens. But she thinks I mean Darryl. She too, is hypnotized by guns.

I climb into the closet.

I wait. There are muffled voices far off. Darryl and the real cop, in the kitchen. And then the sound of the cop coming down the hall. His heavy footsteps, "Hello? Hernandez? That you in here? O'Connor?"

When the door to the spare room opens, I leap out.

I've taken out the taser from my belt, and now the taser is at the cop's throat. I pull the trigger on the taser, the fat cop collapses on the floor.

I'm able to handcuff him, arms behind his back. Into the closet he goes.

Allison is hiding in the shower. "Its safe now, let's go."

She takes my hand and follows me out the sliding glass door, confused.

"Ah look at that!" I say. There, through the canopy of trees, "That's my old friend, the dumb sun. My shift is just about over."

I'm holding a rubber gun in my left hand and a real one in my right, and only notice when my nose itches.

She finds her boots on the edge of the wood line. Already a slug has made its home on the soft leather, but she bats it off and it falls back into the slimy leaves.

We walk quicker now that she is no longer barefoot. But we don't go far.

I have Allison sit on some patio furniture in her neighbor's backyard. I have Allison close her eyes. I say, "Count backwards from 1000 and when you get to 0, you are a free woman and your life will begin anew, don't ever return to the limitations of your old life, the old you has been put on an escalator that is forever voyaging up into the unknown clouds. Isn't that nice? The new you is right here, is right in this very chair. There are no unknowns for the new you. Your life is a glowing orb, forever expanding from the palm of your own perfect hand."

I kiss her hand and she doesn't seem to like that. But she does close her eyes. And she does begin to count.

By the time she has reached nine hundred and eighty one, I am already well into the woods. Leaping over logs and brush like a hurdler at the Olympic games.

As she reaches eight hundred and twenty, I have already reached my place of employment.

At six hundred, I am dressed again in my proper uniform, and though sweaty and winded, I am mopping.

By the time she is at four hundred, her neighbor has looked out the back window and noticed she is sitting in the yard.

By two hundred, more real police are arriving. Their sirens can be heard.

By one hundred, I am at the vending machine getting a pack of peanuts.

By her count of fifty, officers Hernandez and O'Connor are walking into the yard. Soon they are speaking to Allison, but she is not responding.

Her eyes are clenched tight and she is counting down. Seven. Six. Five. Four. Three. Two. She is ready for her new life.

RIP

THE MOVERS COME WITH SOMEONE ELSE'S LIFE. SHE can't tell at first, so she is directing the men to put the boxes marked 'KTICHEN' in our new kitchen.

I'm frantically sweeping up dust bunnies. No money for paint, at least the floors will be clean.

The floors are warped but we'll sleep on them until payday.

She notices the couch isn't ours, not plaid and doesn't have any holes. She calls me from the other room and I walk to her carrying my broom, bottom up like a trident.

"That's weird," she says, pointing.

The movers have placed the couch in the center of the living room, and my wife and I stand there admiring its shiny leather slopes and folds. The artful buttons and fine wooden legs, perfect pieces of driftwood.

And here come the movers with more boxes marked 'BEDROOM', 'BEDROOM 4', 'LIBRARY'.

We point, they go, but some of those rooms don't exist here.

"We should stop them," she whispers.

"We can't stop anybody or anything," I say, leaning on the trident.

Our new home is a 2 bedroom, 1 bath ranch with a yard full of rocks and moss that won't yield grass. The back patio is slimy from excess rain and a terrible blanket of perpetual shade.

Here comes another couch, and another. I have to tell the movers to put some of this fine furniture on the lawn or back into the truck.

The house is an ugly exoskeleton and we are filling it up with ourselves and other possessions.

I'm on 500mg of Welbutrin. I don't care about my teeth or the weather or the re-wilding of the gray wolf; I shrug my shoulders about this too.

She takes my hand and leads me to the kitchen and we open more boxes, ones that say 'DINING ROOM', but we don't have an official dining room—and look at this, the boxes are stuffed with fine china. Powder blue scrolls and gold leaf temples.

I am wondering if these plates are microwavable and, deciding that they are probably not, I am put off. We haven't cooked anything in an oven or on the stove since we were adolescents. We're adults, and are not going to regress back to that regular cooking. We have seen the power of an ordinary $42 microwave. Our god lives in its control panel.

"Do people still call it china?"

"And where the fuck is our microwave!"

The men come with boxes marked 'BEDROOM 2' and 'SAUNA' and 'MUDROOM'.

"Mudroom and Sauna," she says, "What's the difference?"

"We'll never know for sure."

"Put the sauna boxes on the slates outside the screen door, please."

The movers are quick. Just another hour.

We're only able to tip them $5 each, but we hadn't anticipated this. We're meager people. All this heft and bulk and quality of mahogany bookcases and stainless steel espresso machines, the leather bound volumes of encyclopedias, the life size marble statue of the man with his head broken off but his penis erect.

She lets them select pieces of the fine china on their way out.

Then I'm looking at four big screen TVs, all surprises, that I've arranged in a line across the entire width of the narrow living room with the low popcorn ceiling.

The house is quiet then.

We sit on the leather couch, leaning back, sighing deep.

"Probably, this cost more than our car."

We sleep in a sultan's bed, high posted and curtained with fabric as blue as the sea. There must be a million duck feathers tucked into it. Magic springs, craftsmanship baffling. We were all set to spend the night on the air mattress, but the air mattress never shows up. Neither does the microwave.

It doesn't matter, if you opened the door to the microwave and looked inside, it was like looking inside a slaughterhouse. The globs of red stuck to all the walls. Tomato soup having bubbled and exploded, the second you stopped looking.

That night I have a dream that I am swooping over the ocean on the sultan's bed and there are endless sea creatures below, swimming frantically on the surface of the water, mollusks, gastropods, and bivalves, all trying to catch the beautiful shells they have lost, but the beautiful shells are being pulled by tides faster than the pink gummy sea creatures can move.

We don't hear from anyone. No one comes looking for their fancy scuba gear.

Our important things, like our wedding photos and my mother's ashes, were packed safely in the trunk of our Nissan, so we're not missing much of anything that matters. And the things we are missing, are found in the wrongly delivered boxes, and they're certainly upgrades.

She calls me R.I.P. now.

His clothes are all monogrammed and I try to guess.

Ryan Igor Palone.

Robert Ian Piper.

Robert Ike Peterson.

A few of their boxes we throw out without even opening.

One in particular marked 'DUNGEON'.

Neither of us wants to know the contents of the dungeon box.

When she isn't home, I go out in the shed and search some of the remaining boxes for things to give as gifts, or to receive as gifts. Things to set aside for when I forget her birthday, our anniversary, my birthday, who are you, who am I, I've found that the canvas sneakers I used to wear every day are far too small and I'm happiest in these boots of Spanish leather, big as canoes.

The people, whoever they are, liked masks.
There are six boxes of masks.
Some elaborate. Some simple.

She is sitting on the floor wearing a shark mask, pretending to breathe heavy. I am standing on the couch, jumping like a child, because it isn't mine.

The extra couches, forgotten on the lawn, have all been consumed by mice, and moss and centipedes.

"Sharks breathe out their gills!" I say, laughing.

"Well, I don't have gills. All I have is this fake mouth full of daggers."

She takes the mask off and her cheekbones are somehow even more architecturally profound.

"How are you feeling these days?"

"Like someone else."

"Do you think someone in a mansion somewhere is wearing your high school letter jacket, chained up in a dungeon?"

"It didn't fit me anymore," I say. "It's just as well."

Boss

ANDRE THE GIANT ONCE DRANK SIXTEEN BOTTLES of red wine and then wrestled twenty men at once, and won. Well it's all staged, but he was victorious nonetheless.

I got a flat tire last month and my life spiraled out of control just a half mile from the rest stop. I stood on the side of the turnpike totally defeated, no idea how to get the tire off.

I started pulling random things out of the trunk; a big white frame; a box of used books I was supposed to drop off at the shelter; Tracy's travel suitcase bursting with nail polish, toothpicks, her yellow sundress. When the cop pulled up behind me he was laughing because I was trying to loosen the lug nuts with one of Tracy's purple flip flops.

He stopped laughing when I began to cry.

One time Andre the Giant went to the bar in the lobby of a hotel. He drank 156 cans of beer and then passed out. The staff of the hotel, all of them working as a great force of army ants, couldn't move Andre back up to his room so instead they put a piano cover over him and let him sleep down in the lobby bar, undetected. Everyone thought he was a piano.

I tried to convince the cop to help me push my car to the rest stop because the tow bill would crush my wife and I. But the look on his face became even more worrisome, as if he was morphing into an agent of total evil. Sprouting wings, tar black and glimmering in the emergency sun.

"You can't push a car with a flat tire. The distance is too far anyway. What's wrong with you?"

I blurted out, "Four guys were messing with Andre the Giant in this restaurant, saying cruel things and finally he got mad and chased the men out into the parking lot. They locked themselves in their car and do you know what Andre the Giant did?"

The tears streamed down my face and the cop reached for his gun. Or his radio. Or was just scratching his leg. "I don't care what Andre the Giant did, get back in your car … have a seat. Leave the suitcase. Leave the flip flops."

"Andre the Giant flipped the car!" I shouted. "And he could also pick up Arnold Schwarzenegger with one hand!"

An ambulance came for me. The EMTs towered over my little interrupted life, their shadows obliterating me. I kept my arms at my side and didn't move. Like a fragile baby bird fallen out of a tree, I was picked up gently and placed on a stretcher.

To avoid a critical injury from a bodyslam, a person spreads their body out so the impact is dispersed evenly throughout the body. I did the same thing when they lowered me onto the stretcher.

As the ambulance pulled away, I saw the tow truck hook up to the car. Not much was wrong with it. But everything was wrong with it. Inexplicably.

The car and I were separated into the vastness of where sick things go off to be sick and out of sight.

The car was fixed easily enough. I was fixed, too. I stayed in a bed for two nights in the emergency room psych ward and Tracy came and stayed there with me as long as the nurses and doctors would let her.

"What happened?" she whispered when my terror finally subsided enough so that I could blink.

She sat at the edge the bed. The crown of her head looked to me then like it was scraping the popcorn ceiling.

I was shrinking even further. My fingers so thin the rings slipped off and rolled across the floor of the hospital and down a storm drain that wasn't even there.

Heard the sounds of the announcers hyping up the main event to come, but blinked and it was just an orderly pushing an empty wheelchair down the hallway, talking to himself because no one else cared.

I pushed Tracy's massive hand away from mine.

I said, "Tracy! Are you screwing Andre the Giant?"

"What, baby?" Tracy extended her arm to touch me, but I was able to roll and squirrel away in the wrestling ring of the bed.

An hour later she came back with four things: a newspaper with the day's date, May 23, 2016; a print out of the obituary for the man himself, André René Roussimoff, who'd died on January 27, 1993 in Paris, France; a turkey sandwich that was dry and salty but went down with a flood of relief; and finally, orange juice that Tracy had brought from our house. Squeezed from a tree she'd planted for me on our third anniversary, coincidentally Wrestlemania 29. So much pulp you almost had to chew.

To kick off the night, Andre the Giant would drink three cases of beer, eat a couple lobsters—and count them on your fingers—1-2-3-4-5 steaks. This would all be washed down with an entire bottle of Jack Daniel's.

When the night nurse insisted it was time to end the visit, Tracy kissed my eyelids. The tranquilizers let me sleep for the first time in almost a week.

It was like a great black tarp spread across my senses.

No music tonight, come back this weekend.

The next time I saw my wife, she was five foot four again and I was five foot three and one hundred and twenty pounds. I ate an apple and pretended it was an entire Thanksgiving banquet. My stomach couldn't handle much.

Peanut butter and olive oil in everything I can manage, the nutritionist suggested.

"Who do you really want to be?" the lead doc coaxed.

"I'm not sure if I want to be superhuman or just to understand what it means to be human in my own body."

"Rad," the doctor said.

I was released tenderly back out into the unchoreographed world.

A few days later, we were walking along the side of the turnpike, searching the cattails, kudzu, astor, thistle for the place where I'd abandoned her possessions in my state of emergency.

It felt like a lost cause, that walk, the traffic whipping by as we moved forward. Humidity. Sweat soaking through our clothes, as we held hands and fought, locked in a death grip.

"Oh there!" Tracy said, walking into the trash strewn vegetation. There was her yellow sundress, hanging almost vertically in tall grass. I was worried her feet would be pierced by thorns. But she came out just fine.

Over our shoulder there was a whoop whoop and we turned to see the cop climbing out of his car.

"Trouble?" he said.

"Looking for something we lost," Tracy said.

"And what's that ..." the cop said.

My mouth was clamped shut, but the cop recognized me without a word, and he looked happy about it. "Andre!"

I shook his hand, and he waved us over to the police cruiser. A flick of the wrist, a twist of a key, and the trunk of the cop car popped open.

He pulled the big white frame out of the trunk and handed it over to us.

"Sorry though, my dog ate the flip flops."

"Thanks, Boss," I said.

As big as he was, if Andre the Giant liked someone he called them Boss. I am trying to expand in any way I can. I am taking in all the air from the world and filing the flat tire back up.

Tracy's foot pushed down on the pedal. We were in her pickup truck, and it had stopped raining. She had on the red flip flops I bought her to say sorry.

On our way to the party, we stopped at the liquor store. She waited in the truck as I jumped down from the passenger side, sneakers slapping the asphalt. I went into the store and grabbed a six pack of wine coolers for my mother.

On my tippy toes, I leaned on the counter, elbows splayed out. "Need a recommendation," I said to the clerk.

"Who doesn't," he said, and I saw how drunk and weak he was in his collared shirt, hands shaking on the lottery machine.

With confidence I said, "What's the best wine for a guy who wants to drink 17 bottles tonight, then fight 21 men?"

The clerk laughed, "Sorry, doesn't exist."

I laughed too. I said, "I don't even drink."

The clerk said, "I like you anyway."

It was a mixed batch. Clementine. Raspberry. Blueberry. Blackberry. When he scanned the wine coolers there was a happy beep from the register. Instead of change, I took two scratch off lottery tickets and I left the other coins in the jar for the cancer cats, the leukemia kittens, the poor little things, only shrinking more and more into nothing.

Freebird

RIP BUD SMITH, 35 YRS. OLD, DIED TRAGICALLY holding his breath because he had the goddamn hiccups. Survived by his wife, Rae, and his hiccups. Service this Friday at 2pm, and again at 6pm, Riotto Funeral Home, Jersey City, NJ.

My viewing was open casket, but that was too loud. Hiccup. Hiccup. The body jumped in the cheap pine box. Someone called the cops, and they showed up grinning. Death Certificate. Stamped. Signed. Laminated, even. Hiccup. The coroner's laconic testimony piped over the speaker system.

A slideshow of my life played on a small screen. My brother and I battling in the gray snow. Dad with me on his shoulders at the Philadelphia zoo, both of us sunburnt and frowning. A polaroid of my mother holding a polka dotted umbrella over my shaggy little-kid head, the rain soaking her, and me yelling at her—about what? I don't know.

Finally, the casket lid was slapped closed, and the sound of the hiccups diminished enough so that the priest was able to give a talk about how important my friends and family were to me (not true), and all about how I was a good person who cared for others before himself (also not true).

The second service was much the same except Rae cried harder each time I hiccuped. She'd yelled at everyone in between services. Now no one laughed. My mother bit her tongue; my father pinched his hand; my brother put his chair leg on his foot and leaned to the side, the pain keeping him straight. I would have laughed, but I was dead.

They buried me the next afternoon. A stupid day. The casket went down into the soggy ground. They played the song, "Freebird" by Lynyrd Skynyrd. My brother claimed it was my favorite song, just messing around, and everyone believed him. Thanks. As the dirt was thrown on the casket, my hiccups grew fainter. Rae paid a company to mic the casket, a wire ran up to a little weatherproof speaker mounted to the headstone.

She came to visit my grave every Saturday, listening to the hiccups, head bowed, arms crossed low. She pushed the intercom button and said, "Bud, can you hear me? I'm here. I'm here." The answer came back across, more hiccups.

At night, kids from the local high school came and drank beer near my grave and listened to me. They left their beer cans all around my grave, and I liked that. I thought it was cool. Here and there, adventurous kids had sex on my grave. Haha, what a thrill. In daylight, Rae swept the Coors cans away. Picked up the used condoms.

Five years later, the hiccups were gone. Rae was relieved. She moved on with her life, remarrying the next spring. Good for her. Most of my immediate family went to the wedding. Ceremony in St. Anthony's, reception at Marston Crab House. I hadn't gotten rid of the hiccups, really. That neglectful groundskeeper, sick of keeping up with the kids, had dug down and snipped the speaker wire with a pair of garden shears. The intercom was disconnected. Nobody knew that but him.

Nature kept on. My embalmed body broke down. Water seeped in the coffin. Bugs. Bugs. Bugs. I became a yellowed skeleton, hiccuping in secret. There was a new war in the old desert and Rae's stepson went to fight in the war and he came back in a wheelchair. He had new legs by Christmastime, went right back into action. Rae lived in a bungalow on the beach and waded chest deep into warm surf. My brother had a heart attack, but was fine. Took pills for it. Went on a low sodium diet. His beard was white and he was happy enough. He still laughed whenever he heard Freebird on the radio. The house next to my mother's caught fire, and some of their roof went up in flames too. They moved into a retirement village. One night, around dusk, as my mother drank rum and cherry juice, she said to my dad, "I can tell Bud is still an asshole, wherever he is." Dad said, "Sure. I feel it too."

The years crawled on. New presidents. Pop songs. Flavors of soda. Genders. Joys. Pains. Sorrows. Triumphs. Some people left earth. Other people came to earth. My skeleton collapsed. The soggy soil was rich with life, just not mine. Most everyone I knew had gone into their own graves, been incinerated, or were trying to break the Guinness Book of World Records for longevity. I rooted for them all. Fifty years after my death the last of my bones were finally eaten up, decomposed. I was gone completely. It felt nice. Rotted away into absolute physical nothingness, I became a piece of music that nobody could hear and complain about, or enjoy, but at least they weren't complaining, you know? Mist that rolled up the cliffside and wandered through the town but couldn't hug anyone. That was fine, no one liked to be touched anymore. Everything didn't belong to me.

The cemetery got a new groundskeeper, and this one was motivated. With a metal rake and a machete, she cleared the vines away from my grave. As she worked, a wire was pulled from the soil. It led to a speaker covered over with ivy that she didn't realize was mounted to the weathered headstone. Down another foot she found the other end of the wire.

They tell you to hold your nose and drink a glass of freezing cold water without stopping for anything. Find a friend to jump out from around a corner and scare you. Eat a spoonful of peanut butter. Do a hundred jumping jacks. Breathe into a paper bag. Put a pinch of sugar under your tongue. Wait.

Wait.

Wait.

The wire was spliced together, and through the speaker came this sound—hiccup, hiccup, hiccup.

Thank you Mallory Smart, Joey Grantham, Rae Buleri, Jaime Fountaine, Michael Mungiello, Alex Higley, Jackson Frons, Bulent Mourad, Tyler Gross, Michael Seymour Blake, Ben Loory, Kevin Maloney, Nic Rys, Daniel DiFranco, Brian Alan Ellis, Kathy Fish, Robert Vaughan, Michael Gillan Maxwell, Blake Butler, Kristen Felicetti, Aaron Burch, and Elizabeth Ellen.

Rest in peace, my dear friend Chuck Howe, who died laughing on the telephone.

Bud Smith is the author of WORK, Dust Bunny City, and Teenager, among others. He lives in New Jersey.